RICHARD LAYMON

Friday Night in Beast House

Includes the bonus novella
The Wilds

LEISURE BOOKS NEW YORK CITY

A LEISURE BOOK®

March 2010

Published by

Dorchester Publishing Co., Inc.
200 Madison Avenue
New York, NY 10016

ISBN 10: 0-8439-6142-2
ISBN 13: 978-0-8439-6142-3
E-ISBN: 978-1-4285-0821-7

Visit us online at www.dorchesterpub.com.

RAVE REVIEWS FOR RICHARD LAYMON!

"I've always been a Laymon fan. He manages to raise serious gooseflesh."

—Bentley Little

"Laymon is incapable of writing a disappointing book."
—*New York Review of Science Fiction*

"Laymon always takes it to the max. No one writes like him and you're going to have a good time with anything he writes."

—Dean Koontz

"If you've missed Laymon, you've missed a treat!"
—Stephen King

"A brilliant writer."
—*Sunday Express*

"I've read every book of Laymon's I could get my hands on. I'm absolutely a longtime fan."

—Jack Ketchum, Author of *Cover*

"One of horror's rarest talents."

—*Publishers Weekly*

"Laymon is, was, and always will be king of the hill."
—*Horror World*

"Laymon is an American writer of the highest caliber."
—*Time Out*

aymon is unique. A phenomenon. A genius of the grisly d the grotesque."

—Joe Citro, *The Blood Review*

aymon doesn't pull any punches. Everything he writes keeps u on the edge of your seat."

—*Painted Rock Reviews*

One of the best, and most reliable, writers working today."
—*Cemetery Dance*

Other *Leisure* books by Richard Laymon:

FLESH
DARK MOUNTAIN
BEWARE
THE WOODS ARE DARK
CUTS
TRIAGE (Anthology)
THE MIDNIGHT TOUR
THE BEAST HOUSE
THE CELLAR
INTO THE FIRE
AFTER MIDNIGHT
THE LAKE
COME OUT TONIGHT
RESURRECTION DREAMS
ENDLESS NIGHT
BODY RIDES
BLOOD GAMES
TO WAKE THE DEAD
NO SANCTUARY
DARKNESS, TELL US
NIGHT IN THE LONESOME OCTOBER
ISLAND
THE MUSEUM OF HORRORS (Anthology)
IN THE DARK
THE TRAVELING VAMPIRE SHOW
AMONG THE MISSING
ONE RAINY NIGHT
BITE

Contents

Friday Night in Beast House...................1

The Wilds...143

Friday Night in Beast House

CHAPTER ONE

Mark sat on the edge of his bed and stared at the telephone.

Do it! Don't be such a wuss! Just pick it up and dial.

He'd been telling himself that very thing for more than half an hour. Still, there he sat, sweating and gazing at the phone.

Come on, man! The worst that can happen is she says no.

No, he thought. That isn't the worst. The worst is if she laughs and says, "You must be out of your mind. What on earth would ever possess you to think I might consider going out with a complete loser like you?"

She won't say that, he told himself. Why would she? Only a real bitch would say a thing like that, and she's . . .

. . . wonderful . . .

To Mark, everything about Alison was wonderful. Her hair that smelled like an autumn

1

wind. Her face, so fresh and sweet and cute that the very thought of it made Mark ache. The mischief and fire in her eyes. Her wide and friendly smile. The crooked upper tooth in front. Her rich voice and laugh. Her slender body. The jaunty bounce in her step.

He sighed.

She'll never go out with me.

But jeez, he thought, why not *ask*? It won't kill me to ask.

Before today, he never would've seriously considered it. She belonged to another realm. Though they'd been in a few classes together since starting high school, they'd rarely spoken. She'd given him a smile from time to time. A nod. A brief hello. She never had an inkling, he was sure, of how he felt about her. And he'd intended it to remain that way.

But today at the start of lunch period Bigelow had called out, "Beep beep!" in his usual fashion. Alison hadn't dodged him fast enough, so he'd crashed into her with his wheelchair. Down she'd gone on the hallway floor at Mark's feet, her books flying.

"Jerk!" she yelled at the fleeing Bigelow.

Mark knelt beside her. "Creep thinks he owns the hallways," he said. "Are you all right?"

"Guess I'll live."

And the way she smiled.

"Can you give me a hand?"

Taking hold of her arm, he helped her up. It was the first time he'd ever touched her. He let go quickly so she wouldn't get the idea he liked how her arm felt.

"Thanks, Mark."

She knows my name!

"You're welcome, Alison."

When she stood up, she winced. She bent over, lifted the left leg of her big, loose shorts and looked at her knee. It had a reddish hue, but Mark found his eyes drawn upward to the soft tan of her thigh.

She fingered her kneecap, prodded it gently.

"Guess it's okay," she muttered.

"You'll probably have a nice bruise."

She made a move to pick up one of her books, but Mark said, "Wait. I'll get 'em." Then he gathered her scattered books and binders.

When he was done, he handed them to her and she said, "Thanks, Mark. You're a real gentleman."

"Glad I could help."

He stared at the telephone.

I've *got* to call her today while it's fresh in her mind.

He wiped his sweaty hands on his jeans, reached out and picked up the phone. He heard a dial tone. His other hand trembled as he tapped in her number. Each touch made a musical note in his ear.

Before pushing the last key, he hung up fast.

I can't! I can't! God, I'm such a chickenshit yellow bastard!

This is nuts, he told himself. Calm down and do it. Hell, I'll probably just get a busy signal. Or her mom'll pick up the phone and say she isn't home. Or I'll get the answering machine. Ten to one I won't even get to talk to Alison.

He wiped his hands again, then picked up the phone and dialed . . . dialed *all* the numbers.

His arm ached to slam down the phone.

He kept it to his ear.

It's ringing!

Yeah, but nobody'll pick it up. I'll get the answering machine.

If I get the answering machine, he thought, I'll hang up.

Hang up now!

"Hello?"

Oh my God oh my God!

"Hi," he said. "Alison?"

"Hi."

"It's Mark Matthews."

"Ah. Hi, Mark."

"I, uh, just thought I'd call and see if you're okay. How's your knee?"

"Well, I've got a bruise. But I guess I'm fine. That was really nice of you to stop and help me."

"Oh, well . . ."

"I don't know where Bigelow gets off, going around crashing into everybody. I mean, jeez, I'm *sorry* he's messed up and everything, but I hardly think that's any excuse for running people *over*, for godsake."

"Yeah. It's not right."

"Oh, well."

There was a silence. A long silence. The sort of silence that soon leads to, "Well, thanks for calling."

Before that could happen, Mark said, "So what're you doing?"

"You mean now?"

"I guess so."

"Talking on the phone, Einstein."

He laughed. And he pictured Alison's smile and her crooked tooth and the glint in her eyes.

"What're *you* doing?" she asked.

"The same, I guess."

"Are you nervous?"

"Yeah."

"You sound nervous. Your voice is shaking."

"Oh, sorry."

"The answer is yes."

"Uh . . ."

"Yes, I'll go out with you."

I can't believe this is happening!

"That's why you called, isn't it?"

"Uh, yeah. Mostly. And just to see how you're doing."

"Doing okay. So . . . I'll go out with you."

OH MY GOD!!!

"How about tomorrow night?" she suggested.

Tomorrow?

"Sure. Yeah. That'd be . . . really good."

"On one condition," she added.

"Sure."

"Don't you want to hear the condition first?"

"I guess so."

"I want you to get me into Beast House. Tomorrow night after it closes. That's where we'll have our date."

CHAPTER TWO

"Have you ever been in there at night?" she asked.

"Huh-uh. Have you?"

"No, but I've always wanted to. I mean, I've lived here in Malcasa my whole darn life and read the books and seen all the movies. I took the tour *before* they started using those tape players, and I know the whole audio tour by heart. I bet I know more about Beast House than most of the guides. But I've never been in there at night. It's the one thing I really want to do. I'd go on the midnight tour, but you have to be eighteen. Anyway, it's a hundred bucks apiece. And besides, I think it'd be a lot more cool going in by ourselves, don't you? Who wants to do it with a dozen other people and a guide?"

"But . . . how can we get in?"

"That's up to you. So what do you think?"

"Sure. Let's do it."

"Where have I heard *that* before?"

He shrugged. "I don't know, where?"

"From all the *other* guys who promised to get me in . . . and didn't."

He felt a strange sinking sensation.

"Oh."

"But maybe you'll be different."

"I'll sure try."

"I'll be at the back door at midnight."

"Your back door?"

"The back door of Beast House. What you probably need to do is buy a ticket tomorrow afternoon and go in before it closes and find a hiding place. The thing is, they count those cassette players they give out for the tours. They can't be short a player when they go to close up for the day. If they're missing one, they know somebody's trying to stay in the house and so they search the place from top to bottom."

"You sure know a lot about it."

"I've studied the situation. I *really* want to spend a night in there. I think it'd be the most exciting thing I've ever done. So how about it? Are you still game?"

"Yeah!"

"All right."

"But . . . we'll be staying in Beast House all night?"

"Most of the night, anyway. We'd have to get out before dawn."

"Are you *allowed* to stay out all night?"

"Oh, sure. Every night."

"Really?"

"I'm *kidding.* I'm sixteen, for cry-sake. Of course I'm not *allowed* to stay out all night. Are you?"

"No."

"So we'll both just have to use our heads and improvise."

"Guess so."

"Just like *you'll* have to improvise on getting in."

"How am I supposed to do that thing with the cassette players?"

"Where there's a will, there's a way."

"But . . ."

"Mark, this is a test. A test of your brains, imagination and commitment to a task. I think you're a cool guy, but the world's full of cool guys. The question is, are you *worthy* of me."

Though she sounded serious, Mark imagined her on the other phone, grinning, a spark of mischief in her eyes.

"See you tomorrow at midnight," he said.

"I sure hope so."

"I'll be there. Don't worry."

"Okay. That'll be really neat if you can do it. Thanks for calling, Mark."

"Well . . ."

"Bye-bye."

"Bye."

After hanging up, Mark sprawled on his bed and stared at the ceiling. Stunned that Alison had agreed to go out with him. Trembling at the prospect of being with her tomorrow night . . . *all* night. Slightly depressed that she seemed less interested in going out with him than in getting into Beast House. And dumbfounded by the task of how to deal with the cassette player problem.

Where there's a will, there's a way.

Usually true, but certainly not always. He could *will* himself to flap his arms and fly to Singapore, for instance, but that wouldn't make it happen.

He'd taken the Beast House tour often enough to understand the system. They gave you a player as you entered the grounds. You wore it by a strap around your neck and listened to the "self-guided tour" through headphones as you walked through the house. Afterward, you handed back the player and headphones at the front gate. Handed it *to* a staff member.

The crux of the problem, he thought, is the staff member.

Usually they were good-looking gals in those cute uniforms that made them all look like park rangers.

If nobody was watching, you could just walk up to the gate, return the audio equipment (slip it into the numbered cubbyhole in the storage cabinet), then turn around and go back to the house and find a hiding place. Or have an accomplice drop off *both* players on his way out while you remain in the house.

But there *is* a gal at the gate and you've gotta *hand* her the player. They want to make very sure nobody's in the house when they shut it down for the night.

So how can I do it? Mark wondered. There must be a way.

It's just a matter of *thinking* of it.

Bribe the girl at the gate?

Create a diversion?

He lay there staring at the ceiling of his bedroom, trying to come up with a plan that might work. Might work when you're just a regular sixteen-year-old real kid, not Indiana Jones or James Bond or Batman.

He came up with ideas. His only good ideas, however, involved the use of an accomplice.

I've gotta do this on my own, he thought. If I drag Vick or someone into it, they might screw up the whole deal.

So he kept on thinking. The thoughts filled his head, cluttered it, whirled, bumped into each other. They didn't make his head *hurt*, but they certainly made it feel heavy and useless.

Without realizing it, he fell asleep.

He woke up at the sound of his father's voice

calling from downstairs. "Mark! You better get down here fast! Supper's on the table. Come on, man. Move it. *Arriba! Arriba! Andalé!*"

On his way down the staircase, breathing deeply of the aroma of fried chicken, he heard a gruff Mexican voice in his head. It said, "Tape players? We don't need no steeenkin' tape players!"

He grinned.

CHAPTER THREE

Plans and hopes and fears swirling through his mind, Mark lay awake most of the night. But he must've fallen asleep somewhere along the line because his alarm clock woke him at seven in the morning.

Friday morning.

He lay there, staring at the ceiling, trembling.

I don't *have* to go through with it, he thought.

Oh yes I do. I've gotta. If I screw up, that'll be it with me and Alison.

But what if I get caught?

What if I get killed?

What if *she* gets killed?

By now, these were old, familiar thoughts. He'd gone through them all, again and again, while trying to fall asleep. He was tired of them. Besides, they always led to the same conclusion: getting a chance to be with Alison tonight would be worth any risk.

He struggled out of bed and staggered into the bathroom. There, he took his regular morning shower. Afterward, instead of getting dressed for school, he put on his pajamas and robe and slippers. Then he headed downstairs.

By the time he entered the kitchen, his father had already left for work and his mother was sitting at the breakfast table with a cup of coffee and the morning newspaper. She lowered the newspaper. And frowned. "Are you feeling all right?"

He grimaced. "I don't think so."

She looked worried. "What's the matter, honey?"

"Just . . . a pretty bad headache. No big deal."

"Looks like you're not planning on school."

"I *could* go, but . . . we never do much on Fridays anyway. Most of the teachers just show movies or give us study time. So I guess, yeah, it'd be nice to stay home. If it's okay with you."

He knew what the answer would be. He made straight A's, he'd never gotten into any trouble and he rarely missed a day of school. The few times he'd complained of illness, his mother had been perfectly happy to let him stay home.

"Sure," she told him. "I'll call the attendance office soon as I'm done with my coffee."

"Thanks. I guess I'll head on back to bed."

As he turned away, his mother said, "Will you be okay by yourself? This is my day to work at the hospital."

"Oh, yeah, that's right." He'd known full well

that she worked as a volunteer at the hospital every Friday. It was perfect. Many of her regular activities kept her in town, but not this one. For the privilege of doing volunteer work in the hospital gift shop, she had to drive all the way to Bodega Bay. More than an hour away. She would have to leave very soon. And she wouldn't be getting home until about six.

By then, Mark thought, I'll be long gone.

"I'll be fine by myself," he said.

Frowning, she said, "I'll be gone all day, you know."

"It's no problem."

"Maybe I should call one of the other girls and see if I can't find someone to fill in for me."

"No, no. Don't do that. There's no point. I'll be fine. Really."

"Are you sure?"

"I'm sure. Really."

"Well . . . I'll be home in time to make dinner. Or maybe I'll pick up something on the way back. Anyway, why don't you make yourself a sandwich for lunch? There's plenty of lunchmeat and cheese in the fridge . . ."

"I know. I'll take care of it. Don't worry."

Upstairs, he took off his robe and slippers and climbed into bed. He lay there, gazing at the ceiling, trembling, trying to focus on his plans but mostly daydreaming about Alison.

After a while, his mother came to his room. "How are you doing, honey?"

"Not bad. I'll be fine. I took some aspirin. I probably just need some sleep."

"You sure you don't want me to stay home?"

"I'm sure. Really. I'll be fine."

"Okay then." She bent over, gave him a soft kiss on the cheek, then stood up. "If you start feeling worse or anything, give me a call."

"I will."

She nodded, smiled and said, "Be good."

"I will. You, too."

She walked out of his room. A few minutes later, he heard her leave the house. He climbed out of bed. Standing at his window, he watched her drive away.

Then he went to his desk, took a sheet of lined paper from one of his notebooks and wrote:

Dear Mom and Dad,

I'm very sorry to upset you, but I had to go someplace tonight. I'll be back in the morning. Nothing is wrong. Please don't worry too much or be too angry at me. I'm not upset or nuts or anything. This is just something I really want to do, but I know you wouldn't approve or give permission.

Love,
Mark

He folded the note in half and put it on his nightstand. After making his bed, he got dressed. He'd thought a lot about what to wear and what to take with him.

Down in the kitchen, he made two ham and cheese sandwiches. He put them into baggies and slipped them into his belly pack. He added a can of Pepsi from the refrigerator. Realizing its condensation would make everything else wet, he took it out, put it inside a plastic bag, then returned it to his pack.

In the kitchen "junk drawer," he found a couple of fair-sized pink candles. He put them, along with a handful of matchbooks, into his pack. After fitting his Walkman headphones into the pack, there was no room left for the Walkman itself.

I don't need it anyway.

He put on his windbreaker, then glanced at the digital clock on the oven.

8:06

Perfect.

Patting the pockets of his jeans, he felt his wallet, comb, handkerchief and keys.

That should do it.

He looked around, wondering if he was forgetting anything.

Yeah, my brains.

He grinned.

CHAPTER FOUR

Outside the house, he took a deep breath and filled himself with the cool, moist scents of the foggy morning.

A wonderful morning, made for adventure.

He trotted down the porch stairs and headed for Front Street.

In the early stages of making plans, he'd considered trying to sneak out of the neighborhood to avoid being spotted by friends of his parents. Friends who would blab. After a while, however, he'd realized there was no point. He might be able to sneak into Beast House and keep his rendezvous with Alison, but his parents were certain to discover his absence from home tonight. Thus, the note.

And thus, no need for sneakiness. Not here and now, anyway.

They're gonna kill me, he thought.

But not till after my night with Alison.

And if something goes wrong and I can't make it into Beast House, I'll just come home and destroy the note and nobody'll ever know what I almost did.

That might not be so bad, he thought.

It'd be *awful*! I've *got* to get into the house and be there at midnight.

Walking along, he thought about how surprised Alison would be when he opened the back door for her.

"My God!" she would say, "you really *did* it!"

And then she would throw her arms around him, hug him with amazement and delight.

Would that be a good time to kiss her? he wondered.

Probably not. You don't go around kissing a girl at the *start* of a date. Especially if you've never gone out with her before. You've got to lead up to it, wait until the mood is just right.

We'll have *hours* together. Plenty of time for one thing to lead to another.

At Front Street, Mark stopped and looked both ways. Only a few cars were in sight, none near enough to worry about. He hurried to the other side and continued walking east for another block. The barbershop was already open, but he didn't glance in. The candle shop hadn't opened yet. Neither had Christiansen Real Estate or the Book Nook or most of the other businesses along both sides of the road. Generally, not much was open in Malcasa Point before 10:00 AM, probably because that was when the first tour buses arrived for Beast House.

Coming to the corner, he turned right. Though bordered by businesses, the road was empty and quiet. He followed its sidewalk southward. Because of curves and low slopes, he couldn't see where it stopped. The DEAD END sign and the fence and rear grounds of Beast House wouldn't come into view for another couple of minutes.

Almost there.

Then the fun starts, he thought.

But the fun started early.

Two blocks ahead of Mark, a police car came around a bend in the road.

Oh, shit!

Just act normal!

Trying not to change his pace or the look on his face, he turned his head slightly to the right as if mildly interested in a window display.

Mannequins in skimpy lingerie.

Terrific, he thought. The cop'll think I'm a pervert.

Looking forward, he started to bob his head slightly as if he had a tune going through it.

Just a normal guy out for a walk.

He glanced toward the other side of the road.

In his peripheral vision, he saw the patrol car coming closer.

He turned his gaze to the sidewalk directly in front of him.

The cop'll get suspicious if I avoid his eyes!

Trying to seem *very* casual, still bobbing his head just a bit, he glanced at the cop. He planned to cast the officer a friendly, uninterested smile then look away, but couldn't.

Holy shit!

In the driver's seat of the police car sat the most beautiful woman in town—and by far the most dangerous—Officer Eve Chaney.

I thought she worked nights!

Heart thudding, Mark gaped at her. Though he'd seen Officer Chaney a few times at night and admired her photo in the newspaper every so often, this was his first good view of her in daylight.

My God, he thought.

She turned her head and stared straight back at him as she slowly drove by.

"Hi," he mouthed, but no sound came from his mouth.

She narrowed her eyes, nodded, and kept on driving.

Face forward, Mark kept on walking. His face felt hot. He was breathing quickly, his heart thumping.

How'd you like to spend the night in Beast House with HER?

The prospect of that was frightening but incredibly exciting.

21

He suddenly felt guilty.

Hearing a car behind him, he looked over his shoulder.

Oh, jeez, here she comes!

She drove slowly, swung to the curb and stopped adjacent to him. Her passenger window glided down. Mark bent his knees slightly and peered in.

Beckoning him with one hand, Officer Chaney said, "Would you like to step over here for a moment?"

"Me?"

She nodded.

Heart clumping hard and fast, Mark walked up to her passenger door, bent over and looked in.

He'd never been this close to such a beautiful woman.

But she's a cop and I'm in trouble.

He could hardly breathe.

"What's your name?" she asked.

"Mark. Mark Matthews."

"I'm Officer Chaney, Mark."

He nodded.

Though this was October, Officer Chaney made him think of summer days at the beach. Her short hair was blowing slightly in the breeze that came in through the open windows of her patrol car. Her eyes were deep blue like a cloudless July sky. Her face was lightly tanned. The scent of her, mixed with the moist coolness of the fog, was like suntan oil

"How old are you, Mark?"

He considered lying, but knew it was useless. "Sixteen."

She nodded as if she'd already known. "Shouldn't you be in school?"

"I guess so. I mean, I guess it all depends."

"How's that?"

"My mom called in sick."

"Your mother's ill?"

"No. I mean, she called in sick for me. So I'm officially absent today."

Officer Chaney turned slightly toward him, rested her right elbow on top of the seatback, and smiled with just one side of her mouth. Mark supposed it would be called a smirk. But it sure looked good on her. "So you're staying home sick today?"

"That's right, Officer."

"In that case, shouldn't you be home in bed?"

"Well . . ."

He felt his gaze being pulled down to her throat, to the open neck of her uniform blouse, on a course that would soon lead to her chest. He forced his eyes upward, tried to lock them on her face.

"Well?" she asked.

I can't lie to her. She'll see right through it!

"The thing is, I'm not all that sick. And I'm a really good student anyway and Fridays at school are always pretty much of a waste of time and it's

23

such a nice morning with the fog and all." He shrugged.

Eyes narrowing slightly, she nodded. Then she said, "And there are such few and such morning songs."

Mark raised his eyebrows.

"'Fern Hill,'" she said. "Dylan Thomas."

"Oh. Yeah. The guy who wrote 'A Child's Christmas in Wales.'"

This time, she smiled with both sides of her mouth. She nodded again and said, "Have a good day, Mark."

"Thank you, Officer Chaney. You, too."

She looked away from him so he quickly glanced at the taut front of her blouse before she took her arm off the seatback. Facing forward, she put both hands on the steering wheel.

Mark took a step backward but remained bent over.

Just when he expected her to pull away, she turned her head again. "Don't do anything I wouldn't," she told him.

"I won't. Thanks."

She gave him another nod, then drove slowly away.

Standing up straight, Mark watched her car move down the road, watched it turn right and disappear.

"Wow," he whispered.

CHAPTER FIVE

When Mark resumed walking, his legs felt soft and shaky. He seemed to be trembling all over.

He could hardly believe that he'd actually been stopped by Officer Eve Chaney, that he'd gotten such a good look at her. It was almost like something too good to be true. But even better—and more unbelievable—she hadn't balled him out, hadn't lectured him, hadn't busted him or driven him back to school or back to his house. She'd not only been friendly, but she had *let him go*.

Let him go with the caution, "Don't do anything I wouldn't."

What was *that* supposed to mean?

He knew it was just a saying. But it didn't really make a lot of sense when you considered that he didn't know enough about Officer Chaney to judge what she might or might not do. All he knew for sure was that she was a local legend. Since coming to Malcasa Point about three years ago, she'd made a lot of arrests and she'd even been in gunfights. She'd shot half a dozen bad guys, killing a couple of them.

Don't do anything I wouldn't?

"Good one," he said quietly, and grinned.

Still shocked and amazed but feeling somewhat more calm, Mark came to the corner. He turned his head and looked toward Front Street, hoping to see Officer Chaney's car again. But it was gone.

He shook his head.

Continuing across the street, he found himself wishing that she *hadn't* let him go. If she'd busted him, he would've gotten to sit in the car with her. He would've had a lot more time to be with her.

Maybe she would've frisked me.

"Oh, man," he murmured.

But he supposed it was just as well that she'd let him go. Nice as it might've been, it would've wrecked his plans for sneaking into Beast House. He still wanted to go through with that, or at least give it a good try—even though Alison suddenly seemed a little less special than usual.

It's just temporary, he thought. Like sun blindness. After I've been away from Officer Chaney for a while, it'll all go back to normal.

"Eve," he said quietly. "Eve Chaney."

He sighed.

Hell, he thought. If Alison's out of my league (and she is), then what's Eve? Like a grown-up, improved version of Alison, and probably at least ten years older than me. Not a chance, not a chance. The best I can ever hope for is a little look and a little talk. With Eve, it'll probably never be better than what just happened.

Forget about her.

Yeah, sure.

He suddenly found himself only a few strides away from the dead-end barricade. A little surprised, he turned around. Nobody seemed to be nearby, so he waded into the weeds, descended one side of a shallow ditch, climbed the other side, and trudged through more weeds until he stood at the black iron fence.

Beyond it were the rear grounds: the snack stand; the outdoor eating area with chairs upside-down on tabletops; the restroom/gift shop building; and the back of Beast House itself.

He saw nobody.

The parking lot, off in the distance, looked empty.

Now or never, he thought.

After another quick look around, he leapt, caught the fence's upper crossbar with both hands and pulled himself up. The effort suddenly reminded him of gym class.

He struggled high enough to chin the crossbar, then hung there, wondering what to do next. He tried to go higher, couldn't. He tried to swing a leg up high enough to catch the crossbar with his foot, couldn't.

Muttering a curse, he lowered himself to the ground.

There's gotta be a way!

The rear side of the fence, extending along the eastern border of the lawn at the base of a hillside, was overhung in a few places by the limbs of trees outside the fence. Maybe he could climb one of the trees, crawl out on a limb to get past the fence, and drop inside the perimeter.

The limbs looked awfully high.

Climbing high enough to reach any of them might be tough. And if he succeeded, the drop to the ground . . .

He murmured, "Shit."

If only I'd brought a rope, he thought. I could rappel down. If only I knew how to rappel.

Screw a rope, I should've brought a ladder.

He'd heard that there were places where you could crawl *under* the fence, but he had no idea where to look for them.

There were also supposed to be "beast holes" in the hillside . . . openings that led to a network of tunnels. But he didn't know anyone who'd ever actually *found* one.

If only I'd brought a shovel, he thought. I could dig my way under the fence.

If I'd had a little more time to prepare . . .

I've gotta get in somehow! And fast!

He glanced at his wristwatch. Ten till nine. By nine thirty, the staff would start arriving.

He sighed, then hurried back to the street and broke into a run.

The last resort.

He'd intended to hop over the fence. While planning the details of his adventure, it hadn't seemed like such an impossible task. He'd seen people do that sort of thing all the time on TV, in movies, even in documentaries.

James Bond, he thought as he ran, would've hurled himself right over the top of a simple little fence like that.

Shit, Bond would've *parachuted* in.

As Mark ran, he realized that the *real* people he'd observed performing such feats in documentaries were Marines, Navy Seals, Army Rangers . . . not a sixteen-year-old high school kid whose idea of a good time was reading John D. MacDonald paperbacks.

What would Travis McGee do?

The fence would've been a cinch for Travis. But he might do what I'm gonna do.

The new plan was risky. He'd kept it in the back of his mind only as a last resort.

If all else fails . . .

All else *had.*

Nearing the front corner of the fence, Mark slowed his pace from a sprint to a jog.

If anybody's watching, he thought, they'll think I'm just running for exercise.

A car went by on Front Street. He glanced at it,

saw the driver, didn't recognize him. A moment later, the car was gone and he found himself staring at the Kutch house in the field across the street.

The sight of the old brick house sent a chill racing up his back. He knew what had happened there. And he couldn't help but wonder what might *still* be happening within its windowless walls.

Old lady Kutch lived in there like some sort of mad hermit.

There were rumors of beasts.

Of course, there were *always* rumors of beasts.

The real things were probably long gone or all killed off.

But old Agnes Kutch was beast enough for Mark. Walking too close to her house late at night, he'd once heard an outcry . . . almost like a scream, but it might've been something else.

He looked away from the Kutch house and watched Beast House as he ran toward its ticket booth.

Bloodbaths had taken place inside Beast House. Men, women and children had been torn apart within its walls. But the place didn't seem nearly as creepy to him as the Kutch house. Maybe because he'd been inside it so many times before. Maybe because it was flooded with tourists day after day.

Looking at the old Victorian house as he ran

alongside its fence, the place seemed almost friendly.

He slowed down as he neared the ticket booth. Looked around.

Saw a car in the distance, but it was still a few blocks away.

He walked casually to the waist-high turnstile and climbed over it.

Easy as pie.

On his right was the cupboard where the cassette players were stored. It had a padlock on it.

He walked past the cupboard, stepped around the back of the ticket shack, took a deep breath, then raced for the northwest corner of Beast House.

CHAPTER SIX

In the area behind the house, Mark found several metal trash cans, one just to the left of the gift shop's entrance. He dragged it a few inches closer to the wall, then climbed onto it. Touching the wall for support, he rose from his knees to his feet and stood up straight.

His head was only slightly lower than the roof.

This I can do, he thought.

He sure hoped so, anyway.

Not with the belly pack on.

Releasing the wall, he used both hands to unfasten its belt. Then he put one hand on the wall to steady himself. With the other, he tossed his small pack onto the roof. It landed out of sight with a quiet thump.

Now I *have* to get up there, he thought.

Hands on the roof, he leaped, thrust himself upward and forward and imagined his balance shifting, saw himself falling backward. But a moment later he was scurrying and writhing, digging at the tar paper with his elbows and then with his knees until he found himself sprawled breathless.

Made it!

He raised his head. His belly pack was within easy reach. The roof stretching out ahead of him had only a slight slope. A few vent pipes jutted up here and there. Near the middle was the large gray block of the air-conditioning unit, nearly the size of a refrigerator.

He picked up his pack, crawled over to the air conditioner and lay down beside it. Braced on his elbows, he looked around.

Nobody should be able to spot him from the ground. Anyone on the hillside would be able to see him, but people mostly stayed away from there. His main problem would be the back windows of Beast House itself, especially the upstairs windows. The air conditioner would do a fair job of concealing him, but not a *complete* job.

He was lucky to have the air conditioner. He hadn't known it would be here. Making his plans, however, he'd figured that the roof of the gift shop might be the only hiding place available to him.

He'd never intended to stay here all day, anyway.

He lowered his face against his crossed arms. Eyes shut, he tried to concentrate on his plans, but his mind kept drifting back to his encounter with Officer Chaney. He told himself to stop that. If he wanted to daydream he should daydream about Alison.

He imagined himself opening the back door of Beast House at midnight, Alison standing there in the moonlight. "You *did* it!" she blurts.

"Of course."

"I'm so proud of you." She puts her arms around him.

Some time later, Mark heard voices that weren't in his head.

He lay motionless.

Just a couple of voices, then more. Some male, some female. He couldn't make out much of what was being said, but supposed the voices must belong to the guides and other workers.

Soon, they seemed to hold a meeting. After a few minutes, it broke up and the voices diminished.

By the sounds of jingling keys and opening doors, he guessed that people were opening the snack stand, the restrooms and gift shop.

Mark raised his face off his arms and looked at his wristwatch.

9:55

In five more minutes, the first tourists would start heading down the walkway to the front of Beast House. They would be stopping at Station One to hear about Gus Goucher, then entering the house and going into the parlor for Ethel Hughes's story. Then upstairs. There, the earlier portions of the tour took place in areas toward the front of the house. Not until the boys' room would there be a window with a good view of the rear grounds.

The first tourists probably wouldn't reach the boys' room until about 10:30.

Making his plans, Mark had figured that he ought to be safe on the gift shop's roof until then.

Might be pushing it, he thought.

After all, the tour's self-guided. He'd done it often enough to know that some visitors were more interested in seeing the crime scenes and gory displays than in listening to the whole story, so they pretty much ignored the audiotape and hurried from room to room.

Only one way to be *sure* nobody saw him from an upstairs window: get off the roof as soon after ten o'clock as possible. But he didn't want to leave his hiding place *too* early; he needed others to be around so he could mingle with them.

So he waited until ten past ten. Then he belly-crawled around the air conditioner and saw the dog.

His mouth fell open.

The dog, big as a German shepherd, lay on its side a few feet from the far corner of the roof. It looked as if it had been mauled by wild animals. *Hungry* wild animals that had disemboweled it, torn huge chunks from its body . . .

Where's it's head? Mark wondered. Did they *eat* its head?

How the hell did it get on the roof?

Feeling a little sick, he belly-crawled toward the remains of the dog. He didn't want to get any

35

closer, but it lay between him and the corner of the roof where he needed to descend.

Flies were buzzing around the carcass. It looked very fresh, though, its blood still red and wet.

Must've *just* happened, Mark thought. Not too long before I got here. If I'd shown up a little earlier . . .

His skin went prickly with goose bumps.

There didn't seem to be a great deal of blood on the roof under and around the dog.

This isn't where the thing got nailed, Mark thought. It must've been hurled up here afterward. Or dropped?

He found his head turning toward Beast House, tilting back, his gaze moving from the second-floor windows to the roof.

Nah.

A bear could've done something like this, maybe. Or a wildcat. Or a man. A very strong, demented man.

Suddenly wanting badly to be off the roof, Mark scurried the rest of the way to its edge. He peered down. Nothing behind the building except for a patch of lawn and the back of Beast House.

For now, nobody was in sight.

Mark swung his legs over the edge. As they dangled, he lowered himself until he was hanging by his hands. Then he let go and dropped. Dropped farther than he really expected.

His feet hit the ground hard. Knees folding, he stumbled backward and landed hard on his rump.

It hurt, but he didn't cry out.

Seated on the grass, he looked around.

Nobody in sight.

So he got to his feet and rubbed his butt. Walking casually toward the far back corner of Beast House, he removed the Walkman headphones from his belly pack.

By the time he arrived at the front of the house, he was wearing the headphones. The cord vanished under the zippered front of his windbreaker, where it was connected to nothing at all.

At least a dozen tourists were milling about the front lawn or gathered in front of the porch stairs. They all wore headphones, too. Not exactly like his, but close enough.

Mark wandered over and joined those at the foot of the stairs.

He stared up at the hanged body of Gus Goucher.

He'd seen Gus plenty of times before: the bulging eyes, the black and swollen tongue sticking out of his mouth, the way his head was tilted to the right at such a nasty angle—worst of all, the way his neck was two or three times longer than it should've been.

They stretched his neck, all right.

The sight of Gus usually bothered Mark, but

37

not so much this morning. As gruesome as it looked, it seemed bland compared to the actual remains of the dog he'd just seen.

Gus looked *good* compared to the dog.

Gazing up at the body, Mark stood motionless as if concentrating on the voice from his self-guided tour tape.

A breeze made the body swing slightly. Near Mark, a woman groaned. A white-haired man in a plaid shirt was shaking his head slowly as if appalled by Gus or the story on the tape. A teenaged girl was gaping up at Gus, her mouth drooping open.

She didn't look familiar.

None of the people looked familiar.

Not surprising. Though plenty of townies did the tour, the vast majority of visitors came from out of town, many of them brought here on the bus from San Francisco.

Several of the nearby people, including the teenaged girl, clicked off their tape players and moved toward the stairs.

Mark followed them.

Up the porch stairs, past the dangling body of Gus Goucher, across the porch and through the front door of Beast House.

I'm in!

CHAPTER SEVEN

From now on, *staying* in would be the trick. To manage that, Mark needed a hiding place.

He glanced at the guide in the foyer. A heavy-set brunette. Busy answering someone's question, she didn't notice him. He followed a few people into the parlor.

Though not here for the tour, he figured he should *look* as if he were, and try to blend in with the others. Besides, he really liked the parlor exhibit.

Ethel Hughes, or at least her wonderfully life-like mannequin, was a babe. On the other side of a thick red cordon, she lay sprawled on the floor, one leg raised with her foot resting on the cushion. She was supposedly the first victim on the night of August 2, 1903, when the beast came up from the cellar and tried to slaughter everyone in the house. It had ripped her up pretty good. Better yet, it had ripped up her nightgown.

The replica of her nightgown, shredded in precise accordance with damage to the tattered original (now on display in Janet Crogan's Beast House Museum on Front Street), draped Ethel's body here and there but left much of it bare. For the sake of decency, narrow strips of the fabric concealed her nipples and a wider swath passed between her parted thighs. Otherwise, she was nearly naked.

A year ago, taking the tour by himself, Mark had noticed that one of the strips was out of place just enough to let him see a pink, curved edge of Ethel's left areola. He'd gazed at it for a long time.

Today, nothing showed that shouldn't. He found himself staring at Ethel, anyway. So beautiful. And almost naked. What if a wind should come along . . . ?

How? The windows are shut.

Cut it out, he thought. She's nothing compared to Alison or Officer Chaney. She's not even real.

But she sure looked exciting down on the floor like that.

The image returned to his mind of the day he'd seen Ethel with the shred of cloth off-kilter.

Quit it, he told himself.

Only one thing mattered: hiding.

Late last night in his bedroom, Mark had pulled out his copy of Janice Crogan's second book, *Savage Times*. In addition to containing the full story of Beast House, along with copies of photos and news articles, it provided floor plans of the house. He'd studied the plans, used them to refresh his memory of what he'd observed during the tours, and searched them for a good place to hide.

So many possibilities.

Behind the couch in the parlor? Under one of the upstairs beds? In a closet? Maybe. But those were so obvious. For all Mark knew, they might be routinely checked before closing time.

He needed someplace more unusual.

The attic seemed like a good possibility. Though visitors weren't allowed up there, its doors were kept open during the day. He'd heard that it was cluttered with old furniture, even some mannequins that had once been on display. He could probably hide among them until closing time . . . if he could get into the attic unseen.

That would be the hard part. A guide was usually posted in the hallway just outside the second-floor entrance. And even if he should find the door briefly unguarded (maybe if he created a diversion to draw the guide elsewhere), he would hardly stand a chance of making it all the way to the top before being spotted.

I'll at least go upstairs and check it out, he thought. The attic would sure be better than the alternative.

After giving Ethel a final, lingering gaze, Mark turned around and stepped out of the parlor. The heavyset guide was keeping an eye on people, but paid him no special attention. He turned away from her and started to climb the stairs.

Halfway up, someone behind him said, "Is this fuckin' cool, or what?"

He looked back.

The wiry guy who'd spoken, a couple of stairs below Mark, was maybe twenty years old, had wild eyes and a big, lopsided grin. He wore his headphones over the top of a battered green Jets cap.

"Pretty cool," Mark agreed.

"It's fuckin' bullshit, y'know. I know bullshit when I see it. But it's fuckin' *cool* bullshit, know what I mean?"

"Yeah. It's cool, all right."

"Beast my fuckin' ass."

"You don't think a beast did this stuff?"

"Do *you?*"

"I don't know."

"Only one sorta beast does this sorta shit—*homo-fuckin'-sapien.*"

"Maybe so," Mark said.

At the top of the stairs, he joined several people who'd stopped at Station Three. Reaching down inside the zippered front of his windbreaker, he pretended to turn on his tape player.

The guy from the stairs knuckled him in the arm.

"Love this Maggie Kutch shit," he said. "Man, she must've been fruitier than fuckin' Florida."

Mark nodded.

"Name's Joe," the guy said. "After Broadway Joe, not that fuckin' twat in *Little Women*." He cackled.

"I'm Mark."

"Biblical Mark or question mark?"

Mark shrugged.

"First time?"

"In Beast House? No, I've been here a few times."

"Where you from"

"Here in town."

"I came up from Boleta Bay. I gotta come up and do the house two, three times a year. It's like I'm fuckin' addicted, man. I stay away too long, it's like my head's gonna blow up like fuckin' Mount St. Helen."

Mark nodded again, then turned his face away and pretended to listen to his audio tour.

Beside him, Joe's player clicked on.

Around him, people were starting to move toward Lilly Thorn's bedroom. He heard a faint, tinny voice from Joe's headset. Though he couldn't make out the words, he knew they came from Janice Crogan and he knew what she was saying.

. . . *After finishing its brutal attack on Ethel, the beast ran out of the parlor and scurried up the stairs, leaving a trail of blood* . . .

She then gave instructions to leave the player on and follow the replica blood tracks into Lilly Thorn's bedroom.

Joe turned toward Lilly's room, looked down at

the tracks on the hardwood floor and smirked at Mark. "Bloody footprints," he said. "I fuckin' love it."

Mark walked beside him into Lilly's room. About a dozen other people were already inside, listening to their headphones and staring at the exhibit.

Behind the red cordon, a wax dummy of Lilly Thorn was sitting up in bed. Unlike Ethel, Lilly looked alive and terrified. This was how she might've appeared immediately after being awakened by the noise of the beast's attack on Ethel. Soon afterward, she had blocked her bedroom door shut and escaped through a window . . . surviving . . . but leaving her two small boys behind to be raped and murdered by the beast.

Joe chuckled and muttered, "Fuckin' pussy," in response to something he heard on the tape.

What if he STAYS with me?

He won't, Mark thought. He's just doing the tour.

Let's just see . . .

Mark turned around and took a step toward the bedroom door. Joe grabbed his arm. "You gotta listen to the spiel, man."

"I've heard it before. Lots of times."

"Yeah, me too. But you know what, you get new stuff every time."

Mark shook his head. "It's always the same."

"Yeah, the *words*. But not *you*. Every time you

44

hear 'em, you're a different dude so they *mean* different stuff. You pick up new shit, know what I mean?"

"I guess so."

"So you gotta listen to the whole thing, *really* listen. Got it?"

"Got it."

Joe let go of his arm.

Mark, nodding, reached down inside his windbreaker and pretended to turn on his tape player again.

CHAPTER EIGHT

He's just hanging out with me during the tour, Mark told himself. All I have to do is walk through it with him, then he'll go his way and I'll go mine.

Maybe.

Or maybe he'll say we should have some lunch together or why not take a walk down Front Street and have a look at the museum?

That's not what'll happen, Mark thought. Long before anything like that goes on, Joe is going to notice that my headphones aren't connected to anything.

The pretense of being on the tour was only meant to fool casual observers. Mark had never considered the possibility that someone might latch onto him.

If Joe finds out I've got no tape player . . .

No telling what he might do. For starters, he'll probably ask a lot of questions. Then he might report me.

Mark put his hand on Joe's shoulder. Joe shut off his player and turned his head.

Grimacing, Mark said, "Gotta go."

"What's up?"

"Don't know. Something I ate. Feels like the runs. Gotta go."

"Okay, man. Later."

Bent over slightly, Mark walked quickly out of the room. In the hall, he didn't look back.

If he comes with me, I'm screwed.

In case Joe was following him, Mark stayed hunched over on his way down the stairs. Plenty of people were on their way up, so he kept to the right. None paid him much attention. He could hear people behind him, too.

Please, not Joe.

At the bottom, he glanced back.

Five or six people were on their way down, but Joe wasn't among them.

Mark continued toward the front door. He was almost there before he caught himself, remembered that he *didn't* need to use the restroom, and changed course.

"Excuse me, are you all right?"

He turned toward the voice.

It belonged to a girl wearing the tan blouse and shorts of a Beast House guide. This wasn't the husky one he'd seen earlier. This guide was slender with light brown hair and a deep tan. Mark quickly looked away from her and mumbled, "Bathroom."

"The restrooms are around back. Just next to the gift shop."

Nodding, he muttered, "Thanks."

Just great, he thought.

He started toward the front door.

Now I'll have to leave and come back in.

"A lot quicker if you go straight through," the guide said.

He stopped and turned toward her. "Huh?"

She pointed at the hallway beside the stairs. "Take the hall, go through the kitchen and out the back door. When you leave the porch, the restrooms'll be straight ahead."

"Am I allowed to go out that way?"

"Anybody tries to stop you, tell 'em Thompson says it's okay."

"Okay. Thanks a lot."

He hurried past her, past the foot of the stairs, and into the hallway. With a glance back, he saw that she wasn't following him. He was alone in the hallway. He quickened his pace and entered the kitchen.

Nobody in the kitchen, either.

My God, I don't believe it!

Believe it, he thought.

He hurried through the kitchen, but not toward the back door—toward the open pantry.

He entered it. Before he could reach the stairs, however, he heard voices from below.

Of course, he thought. Obviously, I can't be *that* lucky.

The cellar was at the *end* of the audio tour . . . the *piece de resistance.* Nobody actually following the audio tour should be here yet, but some had obviously ignored the tape and rushed on ahead.

Damn!

Starting down the stairs, Mark reminded himself that his plans had never included the idea that he would find the cellar deserted. He'd just figured, if one thing led to another and he ended up *needing* the cellar as a last resort, that he would find other people here and he would need to play it by ear.

It's not exactly a last resort yet, he told himself.

But things happened and I'm here.

In the light from the dangling, bare bulb, Mark saw only four people in the cellar. A young man and woman were standing at the cordon, peering down at the hole in the dirt floor. Next to the woman stood a small girl, maybe four years old. The woman was holding her hand. Off to the side, a husky, bearded guy stood staring into the Kutch tunnel through the bars of the door.

The little girl didn't have headphones on. She looked over her shoulder at Mark and said, "Hi."

Mark smiled. "Hi."

The mother frowned down at the girl. "Don't bother the man, honey."

"It's all right," he said.

The bearded guy turned around and said to Mark, "A shame they don't open up the tunnel."

"Yeah," Mark said.

"I'd love to see the tunnel."

"Me, too."

"*And* the Kutch house."

"Yeah. Same here."

"I mean, that's where half the good stuff happened and we don't even get to see it."

"Well, it's still occupied."

"I know that," the man said, seeming a bit miffed that Mark doubted the breadth of his knowledge. "Maggie's daughter. What I hear, she's as deranged as her mother was. Five'll get you ten she's got a critter or two over there right now."

"Maybe," Mark said. He turned away from the man, approached the cordoned-off area around the hole in the floor, and stepped up beside the little girl. The mother and father looked at him, then returned their attention to the hole.

Mark looked at it, too, though he'd seen it many times before.

Just a hole in the dirt, probably only a couple of feet in diameter.

Can I fit in there? he wondered. Sure. I must. It's big enough for the beasts and they're bigger than me.

"That's where the beast comes out," he explained in a voice plenty loud enough for everyone to hear.

The little girl looked up at him. Her parents turned their heads.

"We know," said her father. "We've seen the movies, too."

"Have you read the books?" Mark asked.

The father shook his head and resumed looking at the hole.

"What're you looking at?" Mark asked.

"What do you think?" the father asked.

The mother gave Mark a tiny frown.

"Waiting for the beast to come out?" Mark asked.

"Please," the man said.

"It might, you know."

The girl, gazing up at him, raised her eyebrows.

"Yesterday," Mark said, "a beast came popping up out of this very hole and snatched a little girl." He put a hand on her shoulder. "She was just your size."

"Don't touch my daughter," the mother said.

"Excuse me." He removed his hand.

The father glared at him.

"And stop trying to scare her," the mother said.

"I'm not trying to scare her. I just wanted to warn her. This big white naked beast actually popped up yesterday and grabbed a little girl no bigger than your daughter and dragged her down into the hole with it."

The daughter looked good and scared.

Her father whirled toward Mark. "Look, kid . . ."

"The girl was *screaming*."

The mother said to her daughter, "He's making this up, Nancy. He's a *mean* person and . . ."

Crouching low enough to look the girl straight in the eyes, Mark said, "It *ate* her up!"

She screamed.

The mother threw her arms around the girl.

The father stomped toward Mark. Red in the face, he stormed, "That's enough out of you, young man! That's *more* than enough!"

Putting up his open hands, Mark backed away. "Hey, hey. Take it easy, okay? I'm just concerned about your little girl, man. You don't *want* her to get eaten up by a beast, do you?"

The girl screamed again.

"We're getting out of here," the mother blurted. She picked up the girl. "You, too, Fred. Come with us right now." She hurried toward the stairway.

Fred glared at Mark, then looked at his wife and said, "I'll be right with you, honey."

"*Now!* He's just a troublemaker. He probably wants you to hit him so he can sue us. Don't give him the satisfaction."

He nodded. "I'll be right with you."

"No you won't. You'll come *now*!"

Fred sighed. Then he leaned in close to Mark and snarled, "What I oughta do, you little fuck, is rip off your head and shit down your neck."

"What you oughta do," Mark said, "is lay your hands on some original material."

Fred cried out in rage and reached for Mark's neck.

As Mark lurched backward, the wife yelled, *"FRED! NO!"* and the bearded man leaped out in front of Fred to hold him back.

"It's all right, fella," the bearded guy said. "Take it easy, take it easy. The kid's just a little wiseass. Don't let him get to you. Huh? Come on, now. Come on."

Holding Fred like a friend, the bearded guy walked him toward the stairway.

With the sobbing child in her arms, the mother climbed the stairs backward to keep her eyes on the situation.

Fred, still held by the bearded guy, started up the stairs. He muttered, "It's okay. I'm fine. You can let go."

But the bearded guy held on.

Near the top of the stairs, the mother halted. In a shrill voice, she announced, "You, young man, should be ashamed of yourself. You're a nasty, horrible creature. What's the *matter* with you, saying such awful things to an innocent little child! I hope your skin falls off and you rot in hell forever! And rest assured, we *will* report you! You'll be out of here on your insolent little ass!"

They resumed their climb up the stairs.

The moment all four were out of sight, Mark swung a leg over the cordon. He hurried over to the hole, sank to his knees, then leaned forward and lowered himself headfirst into the darkness.

CHAPTER NINE

I did it! I did it!

Feeling gleeful and scared, Mark skidded and scurried downward. The slope beneath him was very steep at first. After it leveled out, he belly-crawled forward a little farther. Then he stopped and lowered his head against his arms.

He was breathing hard. His heart was thudding. Though he felt sweaty all over, the air in the tunnel was cool. It smelled of moist earth, but the dirt beneath him didn't seem wet.

I can't believe I made it, he thought.

I can't believe I *did* that!

Damn! he thought. Hope I didn't warp the little girl for life.

He laughed, but kept it quiet so the quick bursts of air only came out his nostrils and he sounded like a sniffing dog.

Stop it, he told himself.

For a while, he heard nothing except his own heartbeat and quiet breathing. Then came faint voices. A man's voice. A woman's. He couldn't hear them well, or what was being said, but he imagined the little girl's father was in the cellar with one of the female guides—maybe the pretty one, Thompson, who had given Mark directions to the restroom.

The bastard was right here.

Well, he doesn't seem to be here now.

He imagined the two of them roaming through the cellar, looking behind the various crates and steamer trunks scattered about the floor.

Maybe he went down in the hole.

That's not very likely, sir. What he probably did was hurry upstairs as soon as you left.

I happen to think he's hiding in the hole. Would you please check?

Then Mark heard a voice clearly. It did sound like Thompson. "All I can say is we'll keep an eye out for him and toss him out on his ear if we run into him. Let me know, though, if *you* see him again."

"You can count on that, young lady." Fred, all right.

"But I imagine he probably took off after his little stunt."

"He *terrified* my little Nancy."

"I understand. I'm sorry."

"I don't know what kind of outfit you people are running here, letting a thing like that happen."

"Well, we have a lot of visitors. Once in a while,

someone gets out of hand. We do apologize. And we'll be more than happy to refund . . ." Her voice began to fade.

Mark pictured them walking away, heading for the cellar stairs. He still heard Thompson and the man, but couldn't make out their words. Then their voices were gone.

I've really made it now, Mark thought. I'm home free.

He felt sorry about causing trouble for Thompson. She seemed nice, and it was his fault she had to deal with the girl's father.

Hell, he thought, she probably has to contend with crappy people all the time. It's part of her job.

What if she comes back?

She won't, he told himself.

Maybe she suspects, just didn't want to mention it in front of Fred.

He imagined her coming back without the angry father. But with a flashlight. And maybe with a pair of coveralls to put on to keep her uniform from getting dirty.

She has temporarily closed off the cellar to tourists.

Standing just outside the cordon, she takes off her tan blouse and shorts. This surprises Mark somewhat, even though it's only happening in his own mind. He thinks maybe she is removing her uniform so it won't get sweaty when she crawls through the hole.

Apparently, she doesn't want her bra or panties to get sweaty, either. Mark can hardly blame her; who would want to spend the rest of the day wearing damp underclothes?

Now she is naked except for her shoes and socks. Balancing on one foot, she steps into her bright orange coveralls.

No longer comfortable lying flat on his belly, Mark pushed with his knee and rolled a little so most of his weight was on his right side.

Why bother wearing the jumpsuit? he thought. Why not just crawl in naked? She can hose herself off afterward.

For a few moments, Mark was able to picture her coming through the tunnel naked on her elbows and knees, her wobbling breasts almost touching the dirt.

She wouldn't do it naked, he thought. She's coming in after *me*, so she'll be wearing the jumpsuit.

But *just* the jumpsuit.

Its top doesn't have to be zipped all the way up. It can be like halfway down, or maybe all the way to her belly button, and . . .

"This is it?" asked a woman's voice.

"This is it." A man.

"It's just a hole."

"It's hardly *just* a hole. It's the *beast* hole. It's how the beast came into the house."

"I'm sure."

"Well, I think you'd feel differently if you'd read the books."

"I saw the movies."

"It's not the same. I mean . . . this is the *beast* hole."

"And quite a hole it is."

"Jeez, Helen."

"Sorry."

They went silent.

A little while later, a male voice said, "I suppose it's all quite Freudian, actually."

Someone giggled.

"Am I being naughty?" the same man asked.

"Shhhh."

More voices.

Voices came and went.

As time passed, it seemed ever less likely that Thompson or anyone else would be coming into the hole to search for Mark.

This is so great, he thought. I've really made it. Now all I have to do is wait here until the place closes.

He imagined himself opening the back door at midnight, Alison's surprise—*My God, you really did it!*—and she steps into the house and puts her arms around him, kisses him.

"HELLLLLLL-OOOOOHHHHH!!!"

He flinched.

"HELLL-OOOHHHH DOWN DARE, LITTLE BEASTIE BEASTIE!"

Apparently, just a zany tourist.

As time passed, he found that yelling into the hole was a favorite pastime of people visiting the cellar.

Every so often, a loud voice came down to startle him.

"Yoo-hooo! Any beasts down there?"

"Hey! Come on up! Ellen wants to check out the equipment!"

"Guten Morgen, Herr Beast! Was gibt?"

"Hey! Come on up and say hi!"

At one point, a woman yelled, "Yo, down there! I'm ready if yer willin'!"

A while later, a man called, *"Bon jour, Monsieur bete!"*

He heard languages that made no sense to him. Some sounded Oriental, some Slavic. Some people who called into the hole spoke the English language with accents suggesting they came from the deep South, the Northeast, Ireland, France, England, Italy, Australia. One sounded like the Frances McDormand character in *Fargo*.

Men shouted into the hole. So did women. So did quite a few children.

When women shouted, their husbands or boyfriends seemed to enjoy it.

When guys shouted, their female companions

sometimes laughed but more often told them, "Stop that" or "Don't be so childish."

When children shouted, some mothers seemed to find it cute but others scolded. "Hush!" And, "What do you think you're doing?" And "Quit that!" Sometimes, immediately after shouting a cheerful, *"Hiya, beast!"* or *"Betcha can't catch me!"* into the hole, kids cried out, *"OW!"* Some squealed. Others began to cry.

A couple of times, Mark heard mothers warn their kids, "The monster'll come out and get you if you don't behave."

Mark listened to it all, sometimes smiling, sometimes angry, often grinning as he imagined himself springing up out of the hole at them.

Oh, how they would scream and run!

Except for the shouts, most of the voices weren't very loud. Some, so soft that Mark couldn't make out the words, formed a soothing murmur. He found himself drowsing off. It hardly surprised him, considering that he'd spent most of last night lying awake.

He fell asleep without realizing it, listening to the voices, his mind often wandering through memories and fantasies but eventually taking a subtle turn into dreams that seemed very real and sometimes wonderful and sometimes horrid. Then a shout would startle him awake. Sometimes, he woke up frightened, grateful to the shouter. Other times, the shout came just in time to prevent Alison or Officer Chaney or Thompson from coming naked into his arms and he woke up aroused and wanted to kill the shouter.

He never knew quite how long he'd been asleep.

Though he wore a wristwatch, he tried to avoid checking it. The more often you check the time, he thought, the more slowly it goes by.

So he waited and waited.

At last, figuring that it must be at least three o'clock in the afternoon, he raised his head and pushed the button on the side of his watch. The numbers lit up.

12:35

He groaned.

"I heard it!" a kid yelled. *"I heard the beast!"*

CHAPTER TEN

"You didn't hear shit," said someone else. The kid's sister?

"Watch your tongue, young lady." Her father?

"I heard it, Dad! I heard it groan! It's the beast! It's in the hole!"

"There's no such thing as beasts, dipshit."

"Julie!"

"So sorry."

The boy said, "It made a noise like, *uhnnnn*."

"Oh, sure."

"You just didn't hear it 'cause of your earphones."

A moment later, the father said, "It doesn't appear that anyone else heard this groan of yours, either."

"It's not *my* groan, it's the *beast's*! And they've *all* got earphones on! Everybody's got earphones on! There's a *beast* in the hole! We gotta *tell* somebody!"

"Is there a problem?" asked a new voice. It sounded like a middle-aged woman.

"I heard a beast in the hole!"

"Really? What did it say?"

"Didn't say nothing."

"Anything," the father said.

"It went, *grrrrrrr.*"

Now the kid's going weird, Mark thought.

"Edith?" Another new voice. A man.

"This young fellow says he heard a growl coming from the hole."

"Haven't heard anything like that, myself."

"You had your earphones on," the boy argued.

"I'm afraid my son has a very active imagination," his father said. "At home, he has a monster under his bed and another one in his closet and . . ."

"Don't forget the green monster in the basement," the sister chimed in.

Thank you thank you thank you, Mark thought.

"But I *heard* it. It came from the hole."

"*You're* the hole."

"Julie!"

"Just kidding."

"Come on, kids. We're disturbing everyone. Let's go."

"But *Daaaaad.*"

"You heard me."

"Don't be too hard on the boy," said the voice

of Edith's husband. "An imagination's a good thing to have."

"But I didn't . . ."

"Ralph!"

"Okay, okay. I didn't hear nothing."

"Anything."

"Dip."

"Julie."

"Have a nice day, folks," said Edith.

"Thank you." The father's voice faded as he said, "Sorry about the disturbance."

That was a close one, Mark thought.

Then he thought worse.

What if Ralph tells Thompson what he heard? Instead of passing it off as a figment of the kid's imagination, she might put two and two together.

They've probably browbeaten the kid into silence, Mark thought.

The chances of Thompson hearing about the groan were slim to none.

But he waited, listening, so tense he could hardly breathe, ready to scurry deeper into the tunnel at the first sound of trouble.

If it's going to happen, he thought, it'll happen soon. In the next five or ten minutes.

He looked at his wristwatch.

12:41

Only six minutes since my groan!

He lowered his face onto his crossed arms, took

65

a deep breath and almost sighed. But he stopped the sigh and eased his breath out quietly.

It'll be all right, he told himself. Nobody's going to come down here looking for me . . . unless I make more noise!

Sounds sure do carry through here.

He wished he'd gone farther into the tunnel before stopping. Too late, now. He didn't dare to move.

Only twelve forty-one. Maybe forty-two by now.

Five hours to go before the house closes.

Five hours and fifteen minutes.

Time enough to watch five episodes of *The X Files*. Ten episodes of *The Simpsons*. You could read a whole book if it wasn't too long.

Five hours. *More* than five hours.

Almost one o'clock, now . . .

I haven't eaten all day!

He suddenly thought about the two ham and cheese sandwiches in his pack. A can of Pepsi in there, too. He felt the weight of them against his back, just above his buttocks. He could get to them easily, but there would be noise when he unzipped the pack . . . more noise when he unwrapped a sandwich . . . and how about the *PUFFT!* that would come if he should pop open the tab of his Pepsi?

Can't risk it, he thought.

I'll have to wait. After six, I can have a feast.

Soon, his stomach growled.

Oh my God, no!

No comments came.

His stomach rumbled.

Maybe no one's there right now, he thought. *Or they're all listening to the audio tour.*

People with headphones on, whether listening to music or talk radio or the Beast House tape, always seemed to be off in their own little worlds.

"Monstruo!"

Jeez!

"Buenas dias, Monstruo!"

That's enough, he thought. He lifted his head, stared for a few moments into the total blackness, then began squirming forward, deeper into the tunnel. He moved very slowly and carefully. Except for his heartbeats and breathing, he heard only the soft whisper of his windbreaker and jeans rubbing the dirt.

As the guy topside yelled what sounded like, *"No hay cabras en la piscina!"*, Mark realized the voice was giving him cover noise. He suddenly picked up speed.

"Don't you saaaay that," protested a female voice. "He think you loco, come up 'n bite you face off."

"He fuckin' try, I kill his ass."

"You so tough."

As the male grumbled something, Mark halted

and lowered his head. He had no idea how much farther into the tunnel he'd squirmed. Another six feet? Maybe more like ten or fifteen.

No way to tell, but the voices from up top were muffled and less distinct than before.

Time to eat!

He rolled onto his side, unfastened the plastic buckle of his pack belt, and swung the pack into the darkness in front of him. Propped up on his elbows, he found the zipper. He pulled it slowly, quietly.

The voices far behind him were barely audible.

How about some light on the subject?

He took out a candle and a book of matches.

Lunch by candlelight.

He would need both hands for striking a match, so he set the candle down. Then he flipped open the matchbook and tore out one of the matches. He shut the cover. By touch, he found the friction surface. Then he turned his face aside, shut his eyes and struck the match.

Its flare looked bright orange through his eyelids.

An instant later, the flame settled down and he opened his eyes.

The tunnel, a tube of gray clay, was slightly wider than his shoulders but higher than he'd imagined. High enough to allow crawling on hands and knees.

In front of him, the yellowish glow from his

candle lit a few more feet of tunnel before fading into the darkness.

He picked up his candle. Holding it in one hand, he tried to light its wick as the match's flame crept toward his thumb and finger. Just when the heat began to hurt, the wick caught fire. He shook out the match.

The candle seemed brighter than the match had been.

Bracing himself up on his right elbow, he reached forward and tried to stand it upright on the tunnel floor. He tried here and there. Each time, the ground was hard and uneven and the candle wouldn't stay up by itself.

He reached out farther and tried another place. Just under the dirt, something wobbled.

A rock, maybe.

If he could get it out, the depression might make a good holder for the candle.

He worked at it.

The object came up fairly easily.

Someone's eyeglasses.

CHAPTER ELEVEN

Mark planted the candle upright at one end of the slight depression the glasses had left behind. When he let go, the candle remained standing. It was wobbly, though. He packed some dirt around its base and that helped.

Then he picked up the unearthed glasses. Braced up on both elbows, he held them with one hand and brushed them off with the other.

The upsweep of the tortoiseshell frame made him suppose the glasses had belonged to a woman. The lens on the left was gone, but the other lens seemed to be intact. It was clear glass, untinted.

Except for the missing lens, the spectacles seemed to be intact. Mark unfolded the earpieces. Their hinges worked fine. He looked more closely. Dirty, but not rusty.

How long had the glasses been down here? A few days? A month or two? A year?

How the hell did they *get* here?

All sorts of possibilities, he thought. Maybe a gal was hiding down here the same as me.

But why did she leave her glasses behind?

Easy. Because they got broken.

No. If you lose a lens, you don't throw away the whole pair of glasses. You keep them and get the lens replaced.

She might've *lost* them.

What, they fell off her face?

Fell off her face, all right. *While she was being dragged through the tunnel . . .*

Mark's stomach let out a long, grumbling growl.

He set the glasses down, reached into his pack and removed a ham and cheese sandwich. He opened one side of the cellophane wrapper. As he ate the sandwich, he peeled away more of the cellophane, keeping it between his filthy hands and the bread.

He decided not to bother with his Pepsi. It would've been too much trouble. Besides, his sandwich was good and moist.

As he ate, he wondered what to do with the glasses. Leave them where he'd found them? He couldn't see any purpose in that. He might as well keep them.

And do what? Take them to the police?

You found them where, young man?

In the beast tunnel.

In the WHAT?

Yeah sure, he thought. Thanks, but no thanks.

But they might be evidence of a crime.

Might not be.

What if I show them to Officer Chaney?

Show them to her in private, like "off the record," and we can work on the case together?

He imagined himself coming down into the cellar late at night with Officer Chaney to show her where he'd found the glasses.

They both have flashlights. At the edge of the hole, she hands him a jumpsuit. She has another for herself. *Don't want to get our clothes dirty,* she explains. Then she starts to remove her police uniform.

Like *that'll* happen, Mark thought.

What'll really happen, I'll end up getting reamed for being down here in the first place.

I can at least show the glasses to Alison, he decided. She'll probably think they're pretty interesting and mysterious.

Done eating, Mark used the cellophane to wrap the glasses.

He put them into his pack.

Then he reached out, pulled the candle from its loose bed in the dirt, and puffed out its flame. A tiny orange dot remained in the darkness. Slowly, the dot faded out. He waited a while longer, then found the wick with his thumb and forefinger. It was a little warm. Squeezing it, he felt the charred part crumble.

He returned the candle and matchbook to his pack, then zippered the pack shut, slid it out of the way, and settled down to continue his wait.

Though he tried to relax, his mind lingered on the glasses.

There hadn't been a beast attack in years. The last two situations had taken place all the way back in 1978 and 1979. In Janice Crogan's books, *The Horror at Malcasa Point* and *Savage Times*, Mark had seen photos of all the women involved: Donna Hayes and her daughter, Sandy; Tyler Moran; Nora Branson; Janice herself, and Agnes and Maggie Kutch, of course. From what he could recall of the photos, he was almost certain that none of the women wore glasses. Maybe *sun*-glasses. One snapshot had shown Sandy Hayes, Donna's twelve-year-old daughter, in sunglasses and a swimsuit.

She disappeared!

She was never seen again after the slaughter of '79.

Had she been wearing *prescription* sunglasses in the photo? Could these be her *regular* glasses? Had she been dragged away by a surviving beast and lost them here in the tunnel? Or maybe lost them while escaping through here?

Difficult to picture a cute little blonde like

Sandy—who'd looked a lot like Jodie Foster at that age—wearing such a hideous pair of tortoise-shell eyeglasses.

Besides, she'd vanished almost twenty years ago. These glasses *couldn't* have been in the dirt of the tunnel for that long.

If they're not Sandy's . . .

They could've ended up in the tunnel in all sorts of ways, Mark told himself. But they obviously suggested that a woman had been down here not terribly long ago. And that she hadn't been able to retrieve them after they fell—or were knocked—off her face. Meaning she was probably a victim of foul play.

Someone must've dragged her through this very tunnel.

Someone, something.

A beast?

They're all dead, he reminded himself. They were killed off in '79.

Says who?

CHAPTER TWELVE

Mark lifted his head off his arms and gazed into the blackness.

What if they're wrong? he thought. What if one of the beasts survived and it's *in here* with me? Just up ahead. Maybe it knows I'm here and it's just waiting for the right moment to come and get me?

Quit it, he told himself. There isn't a beast in here.

Besides, even if there is, the things are nocturnal. They sleep all day.

Says who?

The books. The movies.

That doesn't make it true.

Into the darkness, he murmured, "Shit."

And he almost expected an answer.

None came, but the fear of it raised gooseflesh all over his body.

I've gotta get out of here.

Can't. I can't leave now. Not after all this. Just a few more hours . . .

In his fear, however, he decided to turn himself around. No harm in that. He would need to do it anyway, sooner or later, unless he intended to crawl all the way back to the cellar feet-first.

He took hold of his pack.

Is everything in it?

He thought so, but he didn't want to leave anything behind.

Just a quick look.

He unzipped his pack and found the matchbook. Opened it. Plucked out a match. Pressed its head against the friction surface.

Then thought about how it would light him up.

And saw himself as if through a pair of eyes deeper in the tunnel . . . eyes that hadn't seen him before . . . belonging to a man or beast who hadn't known he was here. But knows *now*.

Don't be a wuss, he told himself. Nobody's down here but me.

Who says?

Anyway, I've got everything. I don't have to light any match to know that.

We don' need no steenkin' matches!

He lowered the zipper of his windbreaker, then slipped the matchbook and the unlit match into his shirt pocket.

Now?

He shut the pack, pulled it in against his chest

and began struggling to reverse his direction. The walls of the tunnel were so close to his sides that he couldn't simply turn around. He didn't even try. Instead, he got to his knees in hopes of rolling backward.

The tunnel ceiling seemed too low. The back of his head pushed at it. His neck hurt. His chin dug into his chest.

As he fought to bring his legs forward, he almost panicked with the thought that he might become stuck. Then he forced one leg out from under him. Then the other. Both legs forward, he dropped a few inches. His rump met the tunnel floor and the pressure went away from his head and neck and he flopped onto his back. He lay there gasping.

Did it!

Would've been a lot easier, he supposed, just to crawl backward. But he'd succeeded. It was over now.

What if I'd gotten stuck?

Didn't happen. Don't think about it.

He still needed to roll over, but he didn't feel like doing it just yet. Lying on his back felt good.

If I'd brought my Walkman, he thought, *I could listen to some music and . . .*

My headphones!

He touched his head, his neck.

The headphones were gone, all right. The loss gave him a squirmy feeling.

Where are they?

He knew for sure that he'd been wearing them when he ran into Thompson near the front door. And he'd kept them on when he went down into the cellar. And when he'd said that stuff to the little girl. But what about after her father went after him?

He didn't know.

He tried to remember if he'd still been wearing the headphones when he dived into the hole.

No idea.

He sure hoped so. If he'd lost them in the tunnel, no big deal; he would probably find them on the way out. But finding them wasn't his main concern.

If they'd fallen off his head *before* the tunnel, then someone might find them in the cellar and put two and two together.

Someone like Thompson.

But she'd already been down in the cellar looking for him. If the headphones had been there, she—or that girl's asshole of a father, Fred—probably would've found them.

I lost them down here, Mark told himself. It's all right. They're here in the tunnel somewhere.

With the small pack resting on his chest, he raised his arms and put his folded hands underneath his head. His elbows touched the walls of the tunnel.

I'll probably find them on my way out, he thought. And if I don't, no big deal.

Someone coming into the tunnel next month . . . or next year . . . or twenty years from now might find them and wonder how they got here and wonder if they'd fallen off the head of a victim of the beast.

Little will they know.

The truth can be a very tricky thing, he thought.

A voice, muffled by distance, called, *"Heeeerre beastie-beastie-beastie!"*

Dumb ass, Mark thought.

"Heeerre, beastie! Got something for you!"

He imagined himself letting out a very loud, ferocious growl. It almost made him laugh, but he held it in.

A while later, he thought about looking at his wristwatch.

But he felt too comfortable to move.

Why bother anyway? It's still *way* too early to leave. It'll be hours and hours.

Hours to go . . .

A couple of years ago, Mark had memorized Frost's poem, "Stopping by the Woods on a Snowy Evening." Now, to pass the time, he recited it in his mind.

He also knew Kipling's "Danny Deever," by heart, so he went through that one.

Then he tried "The Cremation of Sam Mc-Gee," but he'd only memorized about half of it.

After that, he started on Poe's "The Raven."

Somewhere along the way, he got confused and repeated a stanza and then it all seemed to scatter apart . . . *dreaming dreams no mortal ever dared to scheme before . . . scheming dreams . . . dreaming screams upon the bust of Alice . . . still is screaming, still is screaming . . .*

It *had* been a raven. He thought for sure it had been a raven at first, but not anymore. It was still a very large bird, but now it had skin instead of feathers. Dead white, slimy skin and white eyes that made him think it might be blind.

Blind from spending too much time in black places underground.

But if it's blind, how come I can't lose it?

It kept after Mark, no matter what he did. He felt as if it had been after him for hours.

It'll keep after me till it gets me!

Gonna get me like the birds got Suzanne Pleshette.

Peck out my eyes.

Oh, God!

Mark was now running across a field of snow. A flat, empty field without so much as a tree to hide behind. Under the full moon, the snow seemed almost to be lighted from within.

No place to hide.

The awful bird flapped close behind him. He didn't dare look back.

Suddenly, a stairway appeared in front of him.

A wooden stairway, leading upward. He couldn't see what might be at the top.

Maybe a door?

If there's a door and I can get through it in time, I can shut the bird out!

He raced up the stairs.

No door at the top.

A gallows.

A hanging body.

Gus Goucher?

Maybe not. Gus belonged on the Beast House porch, not out here . . . wherever out here might be. And Gus always wore his jeans and plaid shirt, but this man was naked.

Naked and dangling in front of Mark, his bare feet just above the floor and only empty night behind him . . . empty night and a long fall . . . a fall that looked endless.

Mark had no choice.

He slammed into the man's body, hugged him around the waist and held on for dear life as they both swung out over the abyss. The rope creaked.

What if it breaks!

"Gotcha now," the man said.

The voice sounded familiar. Mark looked up. The face of the hanged man was tilted downward, masked by shadow.

"Who are you?" Mark blurted. "What do you want?"

"First, I'm gonna rip off your head."

81

Fred!

Though they were now far out over the abyss, Mark let go. He began to drop—then stopped, his head clamped tight between Fred's hands.

"You aren't going anyplace, young man. Not till I'm done with you."

With a sudden wrench, the hanged man jerked Mark's head around.

Mark stared out behind himself, knowing his head was backward, his neck was broken.

Oh God, no. I'm killed.

Or maybe I'll live, but I'll be totally wrecked for life, a miserable cripple like Bigelow.

And out in the moonlit night not very far in front of his eyes flapped the dead white, skin-covered bird.

"Get out of here!" Mark yelled at it. "Leave me alone!"

"Nevermore, asshole."

A moment later, Mark's neck gave way.

Fred's bare legs caught his torso and kept it.

Apparently, he had no more use for Mark's head.

Falling, Mark gazed up at the swinging naked man and at his own headless body.

Oh my God, he's really going to do it! And I'll get to watch! I don't want to see him do THAT to me!

Then Mark saw the fleshy white bird swoop down at him and realized it meant to grant his wish.

"Yah!" he cried out, and lurched awake in total darkness.

He was gasping, drenched with sweat, still sick with terror and revulsion.

Jeez!

For a moment, he thought he must be home in bed in the middle of the night. But this was no mattress under him.

Oh, yeah.

Better stay awake a little while, he told himself.

He'd heard you can get the same nightmare back if you return to sleep too quickly.

Not much danger of that, he thought.

For one thing, he felt wide awake. For another, he needed to urinate.

Man, I don't wanta do that in here.

Might have to, he thought. I can't leave here till after six, and it's probably . . . what? . . . three or three thirty?

He brought his hands over his face, pushed the cuff of his windbreaker up his left arm and pressed a button on the side of his wristwatch.

The digital numbers lit up bright red.

6:49

CHAPTER THIRTEEN

He'd actually slept *past* the Beast House closing time!

Fan*tas*tic!

He turned himself over. Holding the belly pack by its belt, he started squirming forward through the darkness. Soon, the fingers of his right hand snagged a thin cord.

All right!

He pulled at the cord and retrieved his headphones.

Holding the headphones in one hand, his pack in the other, he continued to squirm forward. He stopped when he came to a steep upward slope . . . the slope he'd skidded down headfirst when he plunged into the hole.

Almost out.

No light came down into the tunnel. No sound, either.

The whole house should be locked up by now, everybody gone for the night.

Everybody but me!

He grinned, but he felt trembly inside.

This is *so* cool, he thought.

Then he realized that his mother and father should both be home by now. Had they found his note yet? Probably.

They're probably both mad as hell, he thought.

And worried sick.

He felt a little sick, himself.

I had to do it, he thought. How else was I going to get a date with Alison?

In his mother's voice, he heard, *Maybe you should think twice about WANTING to date a girl who would ask you to do something like this.*

"Yeah, sure," he muttered, and scurried up the steep slope. Not stopping at the top, he crawled over the edge of the hole and across the dirt floor of the cellar until his shoulder bumped into a stanchion. The post wobbled, making clinky sounds.

Mark went around it, then stood up. It felt good to be on his feet. He fastened his belly pack around his waist, put his headphones inside it, then closed the pack. Hands free, he stretched and sighed.

I've really made it! I've got the whole place to myself!

And about five hours to kill.

First thing I'd better do, he thought, is take a leak.

But the public restrooms were outside. Now that he was in, he had no intention of leaving, not even for a few minutes.

If the house had an inside toilet, it wasn't on the audio tour and he had no idea where it might be.

Might not even be hooked up.

Well, the cellar had a dirt floor.

What if I bring Alison down here?

He imagined her pointing at a patch of wetness in the dirt. *What's that?*

Oh, I had to take a leak.

And you did it right here on the floor? That's disgusting. What, were you raised in a barn?

No, she wouldn't say anything like that. Would she?

How about doing it in the hole?

No, no. What if Alison wants to see where I found the glasses?

Hey, Mark, it's sorta muddy down here.

He chuckled.

She wouldn't *really* want to go in the hole, would she?

Who knows? She might. I'd better not piss in it.

Maybe over in a corner, behind some crates and things.

He took a candle out of his pack, removed the matches from his shirt pocket and lit it. The candle's glow spread out from the flame like a golden mist, illuminating himself, the nearby air, the dirt of the cellar floor, the brass stanchion and red plush cordon, and the hole a few feet beyond the cordon. Just beyond the hole, the glow faded out and all he could see was the dark.

Do I really want to go over there?

Not very much.

Even while in the cellar for tours during the day, he had never gone roaming through the clutter beyond the hole. Partly, he'd been afraid it might be off-limits and a guide might yell at him. Partly, though, he'd always felt a little uneasy about what might be over there . . . maybe crouching among the stacked crates and trunks.

He certainly didn't want to venture into that area now, alone in the dark.

Especially since there was no real *need* for it.

Pick somewhere else, he told himself. Somewhere *close*.

He turned around slowly. Just where the glow from his candle began to fade, he saw the bottom of the stairway. He continued to turn. Straight ahead, but beyond the reach of his candlelight, was the barred door to the Kutch tunnel. Though he couldn't see it, he knew it had to be there.

An idea struck him.

He chuckled softly.

Awesome.

He walked forward and the door came into sight. So did the opening behind its vertical iron bars. From the tours, books and movies, he knew that the underground passageway led westward, went under Front Street and ended in the cellar of the Kutch house.

Agnes Kutch still lived there. The locked door was meant to protect her from tourists.

And maybe to protect tourists from Agnes . . . and whatever else might be in her house. Even though all the beasts were supposed to be dead . . .

You never know.

And so with a certain relish and a little fear, Mark walked up to the door. Level with his chin was a flat, steel crossbar. He dripped some wax on it, then stood the candle upright.

Both hands free, he lowered the zipper of his jeans. He freed his penis, made sure he was between bars, then aimed high and let fly.

When Alison sees *this*, he thought, she'll never suspect it was me.

I ought to make *sure* she sees it.

Oh, my God! she might say. *Look at that! Somebody . . . went to the bathroom there!*

Somebody, Mark would say. *Or someTHING. Maybe the rumors are true.*

And she says, *Thank God this gate is locked.*

When she says that, maybe I'll put my arm around her and say, *Don't worry, Alison. I won't let anything happen to you.*

After he says that, she turns to him and puts her arms around him and he feels the pressure of her body.

Imagining it, he began to stiffen. By the time he

was done urinating, he had a full erection. He shook it off, then had to bend over a little and push to get it back inside his jeans and underwear.

After zipping up, he pulled at the candle. Glued in place with dried wax, it held firm for a moment before coming off . . . and Mark felt the door swing toward him.

His heart gave a rough lurch.

He took hold of an upright bar, gently pulled, and felt the door swing closer to him.

CHAPTER FOURTEEN

Mark groaned.

He eased the gate shut, leaned his forehead against a couple of the bars and looked down between them. The lock hasp on the other side was open. The padlock, always there in the past, was gone.

Oh, boy.

In his mind, he whirled around and raced up the cellar stairs and ran through the house. He made it out safely and shut the front door behind him.

In the next version of his escape, he got halfway up the cellar stairs before a beast leaped on his back and dragged him down.

Take it easy, he told himself. If one of those things *is* down here, it hasn't done anything yet. Maybe it isn't interested in nailing me. Maybe it *wants* me to leave.

Hell, there isn't any beast down here. Who ever heard of an animal taking a *padlock* off a door?

Maybe Agnes Kutch took it off.

Someone sure did, that was for certain.

I could go through and take a peek at the Kutch house.

No way, he thought. No way, no way.

Leaving the gate shut, he slowly backed away. Then he turned toward the stairs.

Just take it easy, he told himself. Pretend nothing's wrong. Whistle a happy tune.

Man, I'm *not* gonna whistle.

On his way to the stairs, he listened. His own shoes made soft brushing sounds against the hard dirt floor. No sounds came from behind him. No growls. No huffing breath. No rushing footfalls. Nothing.

He put his foot on the first stair and started up. The wooden plank creaked.

Please please please.

Second stair.

Just let me get out of here. Please.

Third.

No sound except a squeak of wood under his weight.

He wanted to rush up the rest of the stairs, but feared that such sudden quick movements might bring on an attack.

He climbed another stair, another.

So far, so good.

Now he was high enough for the glow of his candle to reach the uppermost stair.

Almost there.

I'll never make it.

Please let me make it! I'm sorry I scared the girl. I'm sorry I pissed through the bars.

He climbed another stair and imagined a beast down in the cellar suddenly springing out from behind some crates and coming for him.

Silently.

I'm sorry! Please! Don't let it get me! Let me get out of here and I'll go home and never pull another dumb-ass stunt in my life.

Almost to the top. And maybe the beast was almost upon him even though he couldn't hear it and didn't dare look back, so he took the next step slowly. And the next. And then he was in the pantry.

Go!

He broke into a run. The gust of quick air snuffed his candle.

Shit!

But the way ahead had a gray hint of light and he ran toward it. Suddenly in the kitchen, he skidded to a halt and whirled around and found the pantry door and swung it shut.

It slammed.

Mark cringed.

He leaned back against the door. Heart thudding hard and fast, he huffed for air.

Made it! I made it! Thank you thank you thank you!

But he suddenly imagined being hurled across the kitchen as the beast crashed through the door.

Gotta get outa here!

He lurched forward, turned and hurried through the kitchen. By the vague light coming in through its windows, he made his way to the back door. He twisted its knob and pulled, but the door wouldn't budge.

Come on!

He found its latch.

The door swung open. He rushed out onto the back porch.

About to pull the door shut, he stopped.

What if I get locked out?

Doesn't matter! I'm going home!

He let go of the door. Leaving it ajar, he backed away from it. He watched it closely.

The porch, enclosed by screens, was gray with moonlight, black with shadows. It smelled slightly of stale cigarette smoke. It had some furniture along the sides: a couch, a couple of chairs and small tables. In the corner near the kitchen was something that looked like a refrigerator.

Mark backed up until he came to a screen door. He nudged it, but it stayed shut. Turning sideways, he felt along its frame. It was secured by a hook and eye. He flicked the hook up. Then he pushed at the screen door and it swung open, squawking on its hinges.

Holding the door open, he stared out at the

93

moonlit back lawn, the gift shop, the restrooms, the patio with the chairs upside-down on the tabletops, and the snack stand. All brightly lit by the full moon. Some places dirty white, others darker. A dozen different shades of gray, it seemed. And some places that were black.

I made it, he thought.

He stepped outside and stood at the top of the porch stairs.

Safe!

Done with the candle, he opened his pack. As he put it inside, he felt the hardness of his Pepsi can. And the softness of his second sandwich. So he trotted down the stairs and walked over to the patio. He hoisted a chair off the top of a table, turned it right-side up, and set it down.

Standing next to the table, he put his hand inside his pack, intending to take out the sandwich. He felt cellophane, realized his fingers were on the eyeglasses, and pulled them out. He set them on the table, then reached into his pack again and removed the sandwich. Then the Pepsi. He put them on the table and sat down.

With his back toward Beast House.

He didn't like that, so he stood up and moved his chair. When he sat down this time, he was facing the house's back porch.

That's better, he thought.

Not that it really matters. I never would've made it out if there'd been a beast in there.

What about the padlock?

Who knows?

Somebody had obviously removed it. Earlier, the bearded guy had been standing at the gate, complaining about not being allowed to go through the tunnel to explore the Kutch house. The padlock must've been on it then.

Maybe not.

Anyway, I'm outa there.

He picked up his Pepsi, opened the plastic bag and pulled out the can. It felt moist, slightly cool. He snapped open the tab and took a drink.

Wonderful!

He set it down, peeled the cellophane away from one side of his sandwich, and took a bite.

The sandwich tasted delicious. He ate it slowly, taking a sip of Pepsi after every bite or two.

No hurry, he told himself. No hurry at all.

I'm already screwed.

If he hadn't left the note for his parents, he could walk in the door half an hour from now and be fine. Make up a story about getting delayed somewhere. Apologize like crazy. No major problem.

But he *had* left the note and they'd almost certainly found it by now.

I'll be back in the morning.

I'm *so* screwed, he thought.

We've always trusted you, Mark.

Where exactly did you go that was so important

you felt it necessary to put your mother and I through this sort of hell?

We're so disappointed in you.

Sometimes I think you don't have the sense God gave little green apples.

Did it never occur to you that your father and I would be worried sick?

Maybe you should try thinking about someone other than yourself for a change.

He sighed.

It would be at least that bad, maybe worse. What if Mom *cries*? What if *Dad* cries?

All this grief, he thought, and for nothing . . . didn't even make it till midnight for my date with Alison.

Says who?

CHAPTER FIFTEEN

He kept his eyes on Beast House, especially on the screen door of the porch.

When he was done with his meal, he put his Pepsi can into the plastic bag. They went into his belly pack. So did his sandwich wrapper and the eyeglasses.

He turned the chair upside-down and placed it on top of the table.

Then he walked over to the men's restroom. The door was locked. No surprise there. But the area in front of the door was cloaked in deep shadows. He would be well hidden there. He sat down and leaned back against the wall.

And waited, keeping his eyes on Beast House.

Also watching the rear grounds.

Ready to leap up and run in case of trouble.

The concrete wasn't very comfortable. He often changed positions. Sometimes, his butt fell asleep. Sometimes, one leg or the other. Every once in a while, he stood up and wandered around to get his circulation going again.

When 11:30 finally arrived, he went to the other side of the gift shop. There, standing in almost the same place where he'd jumped down from the roof that morning, he began to pee in the grass. And he remembered the dead dog on the roof.

It's probably still up there.

How did it *get* up there?

He tilted back his head and looked at the upper windows of Beast House.

He could almost see the dog flying out into the night, tumbling end over end . . .

Thinking about it, he felt his penis shrink. He shook it off, tucked it in and raised the zipper of his jeans. He hurried around the corner of the building, out of the shadows and back into moonlight.

Much better.

Waiting in the wash of the moonlight, he checked his wristwatch often. At 11:50, he walked very slowly toward the back porch . . . his gaze fixed on its screen door.

Nothing's gonna leap out at me, he told himself. It hasn't done it for the past four hours and it won't do it now. There's probably nothing in the house *to* leap out at me.

His back to the porch, he sat down on the second stair from the bottom.

Okay, he thought. I'm ready when you are.

As eager as Alison had seemed on the phone, he expected her to show up early.

He turned his head, scanning the grounds, looking for her. Of course, the various buildings blocked much of his view.

He wondered if Alison planned to climb the spiked fence.

What if she tries and doesn't make it?

He could almost hear her scream as one of the spearlike tips jammed up through the crotch of her jeans.

Five, six inches of iron, right up her . . .

Stop it.

Anyway, she'll probably hop over the turnstile, same as me. If she does, she'll be coming around from the front of the house.

He looked toward the southeast corner.

Any second now.

Seconds passed, and she didn't come walking around the corner.

Minutes passed.

12:06

Where *is* she?

What if she doesn't show up at all? Maybe she got caught. Maybe she forgot about it. Maybe she never *meant* to show up, and it was all just a trick.

No, no. She wouldn't do that. She *wants* to come. If she doesn't make it, it's because something went wrong.

Says who?

Me, that's who. This wasn't any trick. She wouldn't do that sort of thing.

And then she came jogging around the corner of Beast House.

Someone did. A figure in dark clothes.

What if it's not Alison?

Has to be, he told himself.

The approaching jogger seemed to be about Alison's size, but not much showed. A hat covered her hair and she seemed to be wearing a loose, oversized shirt or jacket that hung halfway down her thighs. Or *his* thighs. For all Mark could really see, the jogger might not even be a girl.

He sat motionless on the porch stair, watching, ready to stand up and bolt.

The jogger raised an arm.

He waved and stood up.

Slowing to a brisk walk, she plucked off her hat. Her hair spilled out from under it, pale in the moonlight. "Hiya, Mark."

Alison's voice.

His throat tightened. "Hi. You made it."

"Oh, yeah. I wouldn't miss this." A stride away from him, she stopped and stuffed her hat into a side pocket of her jacket. She took a few quick breaths, then shook her head. "But I guess I wasted my time, huh?"

"I hope not."

"You knew the rules, Mark."

"Yeah."

"Damn. I don't know why, but I really figured you'd be able to pull it off somehow."

"I sorta *did*."

Her mouth opened slightly.

"I've *been* inside."

"Really?"

"I just . . . figured I'd meet you out here."

"Okay. Great. Let's go in." She started to step around him.

He put up his hand. "No, wait."

She halted and turned to him. "What?"

"I'm not so sure it's safe."

She chuckled. "Of *course* it's not safe. Where'd be the fun in that?"

"No, I mean it. I really don't think it'd be such a great idea to go in. I think somebody might be *in* there."

"What do you mean? Like a night watchman? A guard?"

"I mean more like somebody who *shouldn't* be in there. Maybe even . . . you know . . . one of the *things*."

"A *beast*? How cool would *that* be?"

"Real cool, except it might kill us."

"Then *we* could be exhibits." She sounded amused.

"I don't think we should go in."

"Oh."

"I really like you a lot and everything. It'd be

101

fantastic to go in the house and explore around with you. I mean, God, I sure don't want to *disappoint* you. But I don't want to get you killed, either."

In silence, she nodded a few times. Then she said, "You didn't make it in, did you?"

"Huh?"

"You just figured you'd meet me out here anyway and hope for the best."

"No, I got in. I did. It's open."

"Let's go see."

She turned away. Mark almost grabbed her, but stopped his hand in time.

She trotted up the porch stairs, opened the screen door and looked around at him. "Well, *this* isn't locked."

"I know."

She went in.

Mark hurried after her. "No, wait."

She didn't wait. She walked straight across the porch.

"Alison. Wait up."

She stopped and gave the kitchen door a push. It swung open. "Hey," she said. She sounded surprised and pleased.

"I told you."

She turned around. "You really *did* it. Good *going*, Mark. I had a feeling about you."

"Well . . ."

She came toward him, stopped only inches

away and put her hands on his sides. She looked into his eyes for a few seconds. When she pulled him forward, his belly pack pushed at her. "Let's get this out of the way," she said. She slid it around to his hip, then wrapped her arms around him and tilted back her head.

They kissed.

He had often imagined kissing Alison, and now it was happening for real. She seemed to be all smoothness and softness and warmth. She had a taste of peppermint and an outdoors aroma as if she'd taken on some of the scents of the night: the ocean breeze and the fog and the pine trees. She held him so snugly that he could feel each time she took a breath or let it out.

Though her breasts were muffled under layers of jackets and shirts, he could feel them.

He started to get hard.

Uh-oh.

Afraid it would push against her, he bent forward slightly.

Alison loosened her hold on him. "I'm ready if you are," she whispered.

CHAPTER SIXTEEN

"Huh?" Mark asked.

"Ready?"

Still holding each other, but loosely with their bodies barely touching, they spoke in hushed voices.

"Ready for what?"

"To go in."

"Oh. I really don't think we should."

"Sure we should. I've been waiting for this for *years*. It's gonna be *so* cool. Come on." She lowered her arms, turned toward the kitchen door, then reached back and took hold of Mark's right hand. "Come on." She pulled at it.

He followed her into the kitchen. And stopped. "Wait. I have to tell you something."

She turned toward him. "Okay."

"I was down in the cellar. That's where I hid till closing time."

"Really?" She sounded interested.

"Down in the beast hole."

"My God. *Inside* it?"

"Yeah, there's like a tunnel."

"Wow."

"I stayed in there all day."

"My God. How cool! Weren't you scared?"

"Sometimes."

"So how did you return the tape player?"

"I didn't. I never got one in the first place. I came over really early and jumped the turnstile and hid until they opened the house. Then I just blended into the crowd and pretended to be a tourist till I got down into the cellar."

"Good going."

"I was pretty lucky. I had a couple of minutes by myself, so I crawled down the hole and stayed."

"So *that's* how it's done."

"How *I* did it, anyway. But the thing is, when I came out of the hole, I took a look around. You know how there's always a padlock on the Kutch side of the door down there?"

"Sure."

"It's gone. The padlock."

"Gone?"

"Yeah. And I'm pretty sure it was there this morning. So somebody must've taken it off while I was down in the hole."

"The door isn't locked at all?"

"It opens. *I* opened it, just to see."

"Did you go through?"

"The tunnel? No. I got out of there."

"But it goes to the Kutch house."

"I know."

"Nobody *ever* gets to see the Kutch house. This is the chance of a lifetime."

"Yeah, a chance to die."

"Oh, don't be that way. Nobody's going to die."

"That's because we're getting out of here." Turning away, he pulled at Alison's hand.

She jerked her hand from his grip. "Not me," she said. "I'm not leaving till I've checked the place out."

"The *padlock's* off."

"Right. Meaning we can go through the tunnel."

"Maybe someone *already* came through. From the other side. Doesn't that *scare* you? We oughta get out of here right now. We're lucky we haven't already gotten . . ."

"Nobody's stopping you."

"What do you mean?"

"You can go."

"I can't leave *you* here."

"Well, I'm not going." She sounded so calm.

"But . . ."

"Okay, so the padlock's off. Did you get chased or anything?"

"No."

"See anything? Hear anything?"

"No."

"So as far as you know—except for the padlock being off—the house is as safe as ever."

106

"But the padlock . . ."

"Did you actually *see* it today?"

"No, but I'm pretty sure it was there."

"But you didn't see it with your own eyes. So maybe it *wasn't* there. When was the last time you actually *saw* it?"

"I guess maybe . . . early July."

"I did the tour last month," she admitted. "I saw it then. So that's the last time we can be sure it was on the door. A month ago. So maybe it's been gone for *weeks*."

"I don't think so. That door's *always* locked."

"Okay. Maybe it is and maybe it isn't. But even if someone took the lock off *today*, it doesn't mean they're in the house right *now*."

"I guess not," he admitted.

"Come on. Let's take a look around."

"I don't think we should. Really."

"I do. Really."

"Alison . . ."

"Mark. Come on. It took a lot of guts to do what you did today. You don't want to bail out now, do you?"

"Not really. But . . ."

"Then don't. Come on." She took his hand and led him through the kitchen.

"Not the cellar," he whispered.

"Of course, the cellar."

"Why don't we go through the rest of the house first? Don't you want to wander around and see all the exhibits? I thought that was supposed to be the main idea."

"It was. But this is our chance to see inside the Kutch house. Maybe our *only* chance ever."

"I think it's a really bad idea."

In an oddly chipper voice, Alison said, "I don't," and led him into the pantry.

She suddenly stopped.

"What?" Mark whispered.

"My God, it's dark in here."

"Even darker in the cellar."

"Do you have something?" Alison asked.

"A couple of candles."

"Good. I meant to bring a flashlight. Glad *you* came prepared."

"Thanks." He let go of Alison's hand, reached over to his right hip and slid open the zipper of his pack. When he tried to put his hand in, the headphones got in his way. He took them out. "Can you hold these?"

Alison found them in the darkness and took them.

"Thanks."

He put his hand into the pack.

"Headphones?" Alison asked.

"To make me look like a tourist."

"Hmm. Smarter than the av-uh-ridge bear."

Cellophane crinkled softly.

"What's that?" she asked.

"Wrappers. I had my lunch in here. I've also got an empty Pepsi can."

His fingertips found the matchbook. He took it out, opened its flap and plucked out a match. He snicked it across the score and tiny sparks leaped around the match head, but it didn't catch.

He tried again.

The match flared.

"Now we're cookin'," Alison said.

She looked golden in the glow of the small flame. Mark smiled when he saw that she was wearing the headphones.

"Why don't I hold this?" Mark suggested, "and you reach in and get out the candles."

"Sounds like a plan." She slipped her fingers into the opening, then smiled at him. "You don't have anything nasty in here, do you?"

"I don't think so."

Her hand came out holding a pink candle. "Here's one," she said. She raised it and held it steady, its wick touching the flame of Mark's match.

When the candlewick caught fire, Mark shook out the match. Alison gave the candle to him.

"Thanks," he whispered.

"I get the other one?"

"Sure. We might as well use them both."

She put her hand into the pack again. "What's this?"

"What's what?"

She removed her hand from the pack. And showed him.

"Somebody's glasses. I found them down in the beast hole."

"Really? Can I have a look?"

"Sure."

The cellophane made quiet crackly sounds as she unwrapped the glasses.

She raised them into the light of Mark's candle.

Her eyes opened very wide.

She said, "Oh, my God."

CHAPTER SEVENTEEN

Mark suddenly felt sick. Again. "What's wrong?" he asked.

"They're *hers*."

"Whose?"

"Claudia's."

"Claudia who?"

"You know, *Claudia*. I don't know her last name. That grodey kid. Sorta fat and dumpy. She showed up for a while last year."

"Oh."

"Remember?"

"Sort of." He vaguely recalled a pudgy girl with hair that had always looked greasy. "She was only in school a couple of weeks, wasn't she?"

"Try three months."

"Really?"

"I should know. She spent them all *hanging* on me."

"Oh. She *was* always, like, following you around the halls."

"Yeah. Like a dog. She wanted to be my friend. I hated to be *mean* to her, you know? She seemed nice enough. But *too* nice, if you know what I mean."

"Fawning."

"Yeah. That's it, fawning. God, she was aggravating. She would never take a hint. She never knew when to quit. She would like *invite* herself places, stuff like that. There was one time, I told her she should try to find herself some *new* friends and she said, 'You're all the friend I could ever want.' She was *so* awful."

"And she disappeared?" Mark asked.

Alison stared at the glasses. Nodding, she said, "Yeah. I mean, it wasn't like she *disappeared*. I never heard of search parties or anything. One day, she just didn't show up for school. I figured she'd stayed home because she was upset at me. I'd really laid into her the day before. Told her I was tired of having her in my face all the time and how she was driving me nuts. I was pretty rough on her. But jeez, what're you gonna do? I mean, it was like having a stalker."

"That was the day before she disappeared?" Mark asked.

"Yeah. And when she didn't show up for school, I was really glad about it at first. But after a couple of days I started to feel guilty. I mean, I don't want to go around *hurting* people . . . not even her. So I finally went over to where she lived, figuring maybe to apologize. I'd been to her place once before. It was this grodey trailer over in the woods . . . know where Captain Frank's old bus is?"

Mark nodded.

"Over there. So I paid a visit to her trailer and her mom said she didn't know where Claudia was. She hadn't seen her in three or four days. Figured she must've run away from home. And 'good riddance,' she said. What she really said? I couldn't believe my ears. 'Good riddance to bad rubbish.' Can you imagine someone saying that about her own daughter?"

"That's pretty cold," Mark said.

"I couldn't believe it. Anyway, she seemed to think Claudia had run off to San Francisco 'to live with the dykes and bums.' Those are her words, not mine. 'Dykes and bums.' Jeez." She turned the glasses in the candlelight. Then she muttered, "Guess that isn't where she went."

"They probably aren't Claudia's."

"Oh, they're hers, all right. I mean, nobody wears glasses like these. Nobody except maybe a stand-up comic *trying* to look like a doufuss. And Claudia. You'd better show me where you found them."

"Well . . . Okay. Wanta light the other candle?"

Alison returned the glasses to Mark's pack and took out the second candle. "Need anything else out of here?"

"I don't think so."

She shut the zipper, then tilted her candle toward Mark and touched her wick to his. Her wick caught fire, doubling the light.

"I'll go first," Mark whispered, hurrying past her.

He didn't want to go first, but he didn't want Alison going first, either. Besides, he was the guy. When there might be danger, the guy is always supposed to lead the way.

He started down the cellar stairs, moving slowly. With the candle held out in front of his chest, he could see his feet and a couple of stairs below him. The bottom of the stairway and most of the cellar remained in darkness.

Alison was a single stair above him, but over to his right.

"This doesn't seem like such a good idea," Mark whispered.

"It's fine," Alison said. She put a hand on his shoulder. "Don't worry."

His legs felt weak and shaky, but he liked her hand.

We'll be okay, he told himself. I was down here all day and nothing happened.

Anything could be down here. Crouching at the foot of the stairs. Hiding *behind* them, ready to reach between the planks and grab his ankle.

We'll be fine, he told himself. Nobody's been killed in here in almost twenty years.

Says who?

At last, the shimmery yellow glow found the cellar's floor.

Nothing was crouched there, ready to spring.

Mark stepped onto the hard-packed dirt. Alison's hand remained on his shoulder as he walked straight toward the beast hole. When he came to the cordon, he stopped. Alison took her hand off his shoulder and stood beside him.

"How far in did you go?" she whispered.

"Pretty far. I don't know."

"Want to show me where you found the glasses?"

"You mean go in?"

"Yeah."

"Not really."

"Come on." She unhooked the cordon from its stanchion, let it fall to the dirt, then walked almost to the edge of the hole.

Mark followed her. "We don't really want to go down there, do we?"

"I have to."

"No, you don't."

"You can wait up here if you want."

"Oh, and let you go in alone?"

"No big deal."

"It *is* a big deal. For one thing, it's awfully tight. I almost got stuck."

"So stay here."

"This is crazy."

"If you say so."

"It's just a stupid pair of glasses."

"*Claudia's* glasses."

"Even if they are . . ."

"Maybe *she's* down there, Mark. Maybe it's not just her glasses. I have to find out."

"No, you don't. Anyway, she disappeared *months* ago. If she *is* down there, it'll just be her . . . you know, her body."

"Whatever. Hold this." She handed her candle to Mark, then began to unfasten the buttons of her denim jacket.

"You *don't* want to go down there."

"Mark. Listen. Here's the thing. She knew."

"Huh?"

"Claudia. She knew. She was always hanging on me. She was with me when a guy asked me out. Jim Lancaster. She heard me tell him the condition."

The one condition.

I want you to get me into Beast House. That's where we'll have our date.

"Jim said I must be out of my mind," she explained. "No way would he try a stunt like that. So I told him he could forget about going out with me. After he went away, I said to Claudia, 'Cute guy, but yella.'"

"What did she say?"

Alison shrugged. "I don't know."

She turned away from the hole, took off her denim jacket, hung it over the top of the nearest stanchion and came back. The long-sleeved blouse she wore was white.

"Probably just laughed and said, 'You're awful.' Something like that. But this was only a week or so before she disappeared." Looking into Mark's eyes, Alison slowly shook her head. "Never even crossed my mind. She didn't run away to San Francisco. She came *here*. Just like you. To hide and stay till after closing time so she could let me in."

"She didn't tell you anything?"

"She probably meant to sneak out later and surprise me. But I guess she never made it out."

CHAPTER EIGHTEEN

"Even if you're right," Mark said, "that's no reason to go *down* there."

"It's my fault."

"It is not. You didn't force her to do anything."

"She did it for me. Now I've got to do this for her." Alison bent over and peered down the hole.

"They might not even *be* Claudia's glasses."

"They're hers." She turned her head toward Mark. "Are you coming with me?"

"If you go, I go."

"Thanks."

"You're gonna get filthy, you know. That white blouse."

She glanced down at it, then looked at Mark.

Will she take it off?

"I didn't figure on crawling through dirt," she said and looked toward her jacket.

"You can wear mine," Mark said. "It's already a mess." He gave both candles to her, then unbuckled his belly pack, let it fall, and took off his windbreaker. She handed one of the candles back. He gave her the windbreaker.

"Thanks." She poked the dark end of the candle into her mouth and kept it there, her head tilted back while she put on Mark's windbreaker and fastened it. When the zipper was up, she took the candle out of her mouth.

"Ready?" she asked.

"Not really."

"Look, you stay here. I'll just go on down by myself."

"No. Huh-uh. I'll go with you."

"Just tell me how far in . . ."

"I don't know. Maybe twenty feet. Twenty-five?"

"Good. Wait here. It'll be a lot quicker that way, too. I'll just scurry in, have a look around. If I don't find anything, I'll come right out and we'll have plenty of time to do some exploring and stuff."

"Well . . ."

"Anyway, you've already spent enough time down there. It's my turn."

"I don't know . . ."

She sank to her knees. Looking over her shoulder, she said, "You wait here, Mark. I'll be right back."

"No, I'll . . ."

It came up fast, shiny white, almost human but hairless and snouted.

Alison was still looking at Mark and didn't see it.

But her face changed when she saw the look on his face.

Before he could shout a warning, before he had a chance to move, the thing grabbed the front of the windbreaker midway up Alison's chest and jerked her forward off her knees. She cried out. The candle fell from her hand. Head first, she plunged into the hole as if sucked down it. In an instant, she was gone to her waist.

Mark dropped his candle and threw himself at her kicking legs.

The flame lasted long enough for him to see that she was gone nearly to the knees. Then his body slammed the dirt floor. His head was between her knees and he clutched both her legs and hugged them to his shoulders as blackness clamped down on the cellar.

Gotcha!

Down in the hole, she was squealing, *"No! Let me go! Leave me alone! Oh, my God! Mark! Don't let it get . . ."* Then she yelled, *"Yawww!"*

Though Mark still clutched the jeans to his shoulders, he felt sliding movements inside them. He tightened his grip. The jeans stayed, but Alison kept going. Under the denim, her legs tapered. He felt her ankles. Then her sneakers were in his face and then they came off and fell away and he lay there hanging over the edge of the hole with Alison's empty jeans in his hands.

"Alison!" he yelled into the blackness.

"Mark! Hellllp!"

He pulled her jeans up, flung them aside, then squirmed forward over the edge and skidded down through the opening on his belly.

He bumped into her sneakers, shoved them out of the way, and scurried toward the sounds of Alison sobbing and yelping with pain and blurting, *"Let me go! Please! It hurts! Don't."*

Mark wanted to call out and tell her it would be all right. Even if it was a lie, it might give her hope.

But he kept silent. Why let the beast know he was coming?

Maybe I can take it by surprise.

And do what?

He didn't know. But staying quiet made sense. It might give him *some* advantage.

Though he scrambled through the tunnel as fast as he could, the sounds from Alison seemed to be diminishing. She continued to cry and yell, but the sounds came from farther away.

How can they be faster than me? he thought. It's *dragging* her.

Though his eyes saw only utter blackness, his mind saw Alison skidding along through the narrow tube of dirt on her back, kicking her bare legs. The beast no longer dragged her by the front of the windbreaker; now, she was being pulled by her arms. Stretched as she was, the windbreaker didn't even reach down to her waist. From her belly down, she was bare except for her panties.

It must really hurt, he thought. It must *burn*. Like rug burn, but worse, her skin getting scuffed off.

That'll be the least of her problems. When the beast gets done dragging her . . .

That's when I can catch up.

Yeah, right. And get myself killed. It'll take care of me in about two seconds.

But maybe those couple of seconds would give Alison a chance to get away.

It'll be worth it if I can save her.

Worth dying for?

Yeah. Fucking-A right, if I can save her.

Anyway, he told himself, you never know. It might not come to that. Anything can happen.

One of his hands slid over something slippery in the dirt. Her panties? The way she was being dragged, she'd been sure to lose them. Mark snatched up the skimpy garment, stuffed it inside his shirt and kept on scrambling forward.

The sounds from Alison seemed farther away than ever.

He tried to pick up speed.

What if they lose me?

According to the books and movies, there might be a network of tunnels behind Beast House, going all the way out past its fence and into the hills.

What if it really is some sort of maze?

The thing drags her off into side tunnels and loses me, I might have a chance of living through the night.

So far, the tunnel seemed mostly straight but with minor bends and slopes sometimes. If other tunnels had intersected with it, Mark hadn't noticed.

Though the sounds were far away, they still seemed to come from in front of him.

That's a good sign, he thought.

Sure it is. Good for who?

And a voice whispered in his mind, *I don't have to keep going. I can stop right now. Turn around and go back to the cellar and get the hell out. Let the cops take care of it.*

Better yet, don't tell anyone. Nobody has to know about any of this.

"Yeah, right," he muttered.

And kept on through the darkness, out of breath, heart thundering, every muscle aching, his clothes clinging with sweat, his hair plastered to his scalp, sweat running down his face.

I can't keep this up forever, he thought.

So quit. That's what you want to do.

I don't want to quit, just slow down.

He stopped.

Just for a second.

Lying on his belly, head up, elbows planted in the dirt, he wheezed for air and blinked sweat out of his eyes and gazed into the blackness.

He couldn't hear Alison anymore.

It doesn't mean I lost her, he told himself. Maybe she stopped crying and yelling. Maybe she passed out.

In his mind, he saw her stretched out limp on her back, being dragged by her wrists, the windbreaker even higher than before so that she is bare from the midriff down. Her panties are gone. Mark can see between her thighs. Her legs bounce as she is dragged over the rough dirt of the tunnel floor.

"ALISON!" he shouted.

No answer came.

CHAPTER NINETEEN

Mark wished he hadn't yelled. His shout had probably carried through the whole length of the tunnel.

I can't hear them, he thought, so maybe they didn't hear me.

What if they're just being quiet?

And it heard me.

In his mind, he saw the beast slither over Alison's limp body and come scurrying back through the tunnel.

Get the hell out!

He shoved himself up to his hands and knees, but the back of his head struck the dirt ceiling. He dropped flat.

Even if he *could* turn himself around, he knew he had no chance of outracing the beast.

It'll be on me any second!

He listened. Silence except for his own heartbeat and gasping.

He would never see it coming. Not down here.

Even something dead white would be invisible in such darkness. But he would hear its doglike snuffs and growls.

So far, he heard only himself.

What if it's still dragging Alison and they're getting farther and farther away?

Mark started squirming forward again.

Might as well, he thought. If it's coming, it'll get me anyway.

He picked up speed.

Get it over with.

In his mind, he saw himself and the beast scurrying straight toward each other through the tight tunnel like a couple of locomotives.

It's a locomotive, he thought. *I'm* a dog on the tracks.

He remembered the dog on the roof of the gift shop. Disemboweled and headless.

Is that how I'll end up? Or Alison?

As the tunnel began sloping upward, he wondered what was taking the beast so long.

Should've gotten here by now.

Maybe it *isn't* coming.

He struggled up the incline. All his muscles ached and trembled. His clothes felt soaked. Sweat poured down his face, stung his eyes.

And he saw gray.

Not actual light, but a hint of darkness that wasn't totally black.

He made his way toward it, shoving with his

elbows and knees and the toes of his shoes at the hard dirt floor of the tunnel and forcing himself forward, higher, closer to the gray.

Then he noticed a breath of air that smelled like fog and sea, that cooled the sweat on his face.

A way out?

That's why he'd stopped hearing Alison. That's why the beast hadn't come to get him . . . it hadn't heard his shout.

They aren't in the tunnel anymore!

And now the gray tunnel in front of Mark seemed to slant straight up. He tried to climb it, skidded backward, then got to his feet. Standing, he reached up and found rough, cool surfaces of rock.

He found handholds and started to climb. Soon, he was surrounded by large blocks of stone. Surrounded *and* covered. Looking up, he couldn't see the sky. But he did see a patch of pale, misty light from an area eight or ten feet above his head.

He climbed toward it, moving as fast as he dared up the craggy wall.

Hard to believe that the beast had made such an ascent dragging—or carrying—Alison. But it had somehow dragged her with great speed through the entire length of the tunnel. If it was capable of that, he supposed it could do this.

Boosting himself over a rough edge, he found the opening in front of him. Not much. The size of a small window. But big enough.

127

He clambered toward it.

Beyond it, the night looked pale and fuzzy. Moonlit fog?

He crouched just inside the opening and peered out. Through the fog, he could see an upward slope of ground and he knew where he was; at the back of a rock outcropping just beyond the Beast House fence, a short distance up the hillside. He'd seen it many times. Never from the inside, though. Until now.

Outside, trees and rocks looked soft and blurry. Nothing moved.

Where *are* they?

He stood up and saw the beast behind a thicket off to the left. Just its head and back, nearly invisible in the fog. It was hunched over as if busy with someone out of sight on the ground.

Mark crouched. Head down, he searched the area near his feet and found a good chunk of rock. It filled his hand. It felt heavy and had rough edges. Keeping it, he stayed low and hurried in the direction of the beast.

He didn't try to look at it again. If he could see it, it could see him. But he knew where it was. And he listened.

His shoes made hardly any noise at all as he hurried over the rocks and the long damp grass. The night seemed oddly still. All the usual sounds were muffled by the fog. Somewhere, an owl hooted. From far away came the low, lonely tones of a fog horn. He thought he could hear the distant surf, but wasn't sure.

Turning his head to the left, he looked downward and saw the back fence of Beast House with its row of iron spikes. Beyond the fence, there was only fog. Beast House was there, buried somewhere in the grayness. As he tried to glimpse it, he heard a snuffling sound.

Then a whimper.

He hurried on.

The sounds became more distinct. Moans and growls, panting sounds, whimpers and sharp outcries.

Some came from Alison.

She's alive!

But, oh God, what's the damn thing doing to her?

Though Mark knew he must be very close to them, they remained out of sight. The beast had chosen a very well-concealed place for his session with Alison. It seemed completely surrounded by thickets and boulders.

Mark climbed a waist-high rock and looked down at them.

The monster, white as a snowman in the moonlit fog, was down on its knees, hunkered over Alison's back, thrusting into her. Her clothes were gone, scattered nearby. She still wore her white socks, but nothing else.

She was on her knees, drooping forward. She looked as if she would fall on her face except for the creature's hands that seemed to be clutching her breasts. Each time it rammed into Alison, her entire body shook and she made a noise like a dog getting kicked.

Mark leaped off the boulder.

The beast turned its head. Its eyes found him, but they didn't go wide with surprise. They stayed half shut. The beast seemed blasé about this human running toward it with an upraised rock.

But it very quickly stood up, still embedded in Alison, hoisting her off her knees and swiveling, letting go of her breasts and clutching her hips as she swung so that her head and torso swept downward and crashed against Mark, knocking him off his feet.

He slammed against the ground, rocks pounding his buttocks and back, one bashing his head. He heard the *thonk*! Felt a blast inside his skull. Saw bright red. Smelled something tinny like blood. Barely conscious, he gazed up at Alison.

She loomed above him. The beast's long, clawed fingers were clutching the sides of her rib cage, holding her like a life-sized, beautiful doll, working her forward and back.

Her chest and belly were striped with scratches, with gouges. Wetness fell off her and pattered onto Mark.

Her arms hung down as if reaching for him. But they weren't reaching, they were limp and swinging. Her head wobbled. Her hair, hanging down her brow and cheeks, swayed with the motions of her body. Her small breasts, nipples pointing down at Mark, jiggled and shook as the beast jerked her forward and back.

She sniffled and sobbed. She let out a hurt yelp each time the beast jerked her toward it, plunging in deeper.

Mark raised his head.

The beast kept on working Alison.

Mark couldn't see much of it. Just its hands with their long white fingers and dark claws clamping both sides of Alison's rib cage. And its muscular white legs between Alison's legs.

Alison's legs were dangling, her feet off the ground. They gave a little lurch each time the beast rammed in. Through her sobbing and yelps and the beast's grunting, Mark could hear her buttocks smacking against the creature.

Smacking faster and faster.

The beast, grunting with each thrust, worked her forward and backward with increasing speed and power. Alison's arms and legs flopped about. Her hair swung. Her breasts lurched. Her yelps came faster.

It's killing her!

Mark's hands were empty. He turned his head and saw rocks nearby. He stretched his arm out and grabbed one and brought it closer to his side.

Above him, Alison's head flew backward. Mark thought the beast had tugged her hair, but its hands remained on her rib cage as it furiously slammed into her. Her head stayed back. Her mouth gaped. She gasped, *"AH-AH-AH!"* And then her arms stopped flapping. They bent at the elbows and she clutched her own leaping breasts and massaged them, squeezed them, tugged her nipples.

CHAPTER TWENTY

What's she doing?

Mark *knew* what she was doing. Appalled, excited, he watched her growing frenzy.

All wrong, he thought. So wrong.

When the beast came, Alison's whole body twitched and bounced and she cried out and Mark was pretty sure she was having a climax of her own.

For a while afterward, the beast kept her in position. Her head and arms and legs hung limp. She hardly moved at all except to pant for breath. Then the creature eased her forward and upward. Its thick shaft appeared between her legs, and Mark saw it slide out of her.

Bending over, the beast lowered Alison toward him.

Does it think I'm dead?

Mark lay perfectly still as it put Alison on top of him. Her chest, hot and wet and heaving, covered his face. Hardly able to breathe, he turned his head to the side.

And waited.

Nothing happened.

Alison stayed on top of him, done in as if she'd just finished running a mile-long gauntlet.

But the beast did nothing.

What's it doing, watching us?

Just play dead, Mark told himself. If I make any sort of move at all, it'll probably drag Alison off me and rip me apart.

Though her moisture had soaked through Mark's shirt almost immediately, he soon felt a heavy warmth spreading out near his waist. It seemed to come from Alison, from between her legs.

My God, she's bleeding to death!

But the fluid felt thicker than blood.

Mark suddenly knew what it was.

It spread over his belly, rolled down his sides, soaked through his jeans so he could feel its warmth on his leg.

Must be a gallon of it.

As he lay there motionless, the night air turned the semen chilly. But it still felt warm where Alison's body was on top of him.

How long had she been there? Five minutes? Ten? Maybe longer. During that time, Mark had seen and heard nothing from the beast.

He felt Alison raise herself slightly.

"Don't move," he whispered.

"Huh?"

"Play dead."

"But it's gone."

"Huh?"

"It went away . . . a long time ago." Trembling, she scooted herself down Mark's body. She flinched and made hurt sounds. She said, "Ugh." Then her face was above his, her hair hanging toward him much as it had done when she was higher above him in the clutches of the beast. Now, however, she was nearly motionless and her hair hardly moved at all. He wished he could see her face, but it was masked by shadow.

"You came after me," she said.

"Didn't do much good."

"You tried."

Her head slowly lowered. It tilted slightly to the side. She whispered, "Thank you." Then her mouth pushed softly against his mouth. Her lips were warm and wet and open.

We need to get away, Mark thought. It might come back.

But Alison was on top of him and kissing him and naked. He didn't want *that* to stop. He could feel her breasts through the damp front of his shirt. He could feel her rib cage and belly and groin and he was growing hard inside his wet jeans.

She lifted her face.

"We'd better get out of here," Mark whispered. "It might come back."

"Don't worry." Sitting on him, her buttocks on

the soaked front of his jeans and heavy on his erection, she leaned forward and began to unbutton his shirt.

"What're you doing?"

She spread his shirt open, then eased herself down. Almost on top of him, she paused and swayed, brushing her nipples against his chest. Then she sank onto him, smooth and bare all the way down to Mark's waist. Her skin felt chilly at first, then warm. She kissed him again.

Has she lost her mind?

But the feel of her . . .

This was what Mark had always wanted, to have her like this, naked and eager. And how great to have it happening in the tall damp grass of a hillside late at night in the silence and the fog!

She pushed herself up.

"We've gotta go," Mark said.

She started scooting backward. "What's the hurry?"

"It'll come back and kill us."

"I don't think so."

"It *will*!"

"Why would it do that?"

"It's the *beast*!"

A corner of Alison's mouth curled up. "If it wanted to kill us, why didn't it?"

"I don't know."

"Neither do I," she said. Squatting over Mark's

thighs, she bent down and unbuckled his belt. "But here we are, and it's gone."

He pushed himself up to his elbows and looked around. The hillside and boulders and trees looked soft in the pale fog.

"It's gone," Alison said again. She unbuttoned the waistband of his jeans, pulled down the zipper.

Some of Mark's tightness eased.

I can't believe this is happening.

"Maybe it got what it wanted," Alison said. Scuttling backward on her knees, she tugged at Mark's jeans. He raised his rump off the ground. His jeans and underwear slid out from under him.

He was free and rigid in the moist night air.

"Now it's our turn," Alison told him.

"But it *raped* you! It . . . it dragged you away and . . . look at you, you're all scratched and torn up . . . It . . . it *fucked* you!"

"It sure did," she said. Crawling over him, she whispered, "And we never breathe a word about this to anyone."

"We've got to! You're all ruined!"

"I'll heal."

"We've *gotta* tell."

"Never. It'll be our secret. Just between you and me. *Everything* about tonight. Promise."

Mark shook his head.

"Do you want me?" she whispered.

He nodded.

"Then promise."

"But . . ."

She eased down and he felt a soft wet opening push against the head of his erection. It nudged him. He felt himself go in half an inch. Then she withdrew.

"Promise me, Mark."

"What'll you tell your parents?"

"Nothing."

"But you're all messed up."

"Most of it won't show when my clothes are on. If they notice anything, I'll say I crashed my bike."

"But . . ."

"Promise?"

"Okay."

"Cross your heart and hope to die?"

"Yes."

"Cross mine." She moved forward and down so her chest was above his mouth. "Use your tongue."

He licked an X on the skin of her chest, tasting sweat and blood, feeling the furrows of scratches.

"Hope to die?" she asked.

"Yes."

"Okay then." She eased herself down and backward and Mark felt himself slide in. She was warm in there. Warm and slippery and snug.

He knew the beast had been in before him, plundering her, flooding her. He'd heard crude guys talk about "sloppy seconds" and he guessed that was what he was getting but he didn't mind very much.

Didn't mind at all, come to think of it.

CHAPTER TWENTY-ONE

Near dawn, wearing what remained of their clothes, they made their way down the hillside. They stayed just outside the back fence and followed it. Alison could hardly walk. Mark held her. Sometimes, he picked her up and carried her for a while.

They came out of the field near some homes. Except for a few porch lights, nearly all the houses were dark.

They saw a cat. Once, a car went by a block away and they hid behind a tree. They saw no people anywhere. Only each other.

Soon, they arrived at Alison's house. All the windows were dark. So was the porch.

"I left the back door unlocked," she whispered.

They went around the house. On the stoop outside the back door, Alison took off Mark's windbreaker and gave it back to him. Her white shirt was tattered, one sleeve missing and her right breast poking out through a split. Her legs were bare all the way down to her white socks.

"Are you sure you'll be all right?" Mark whispered.

"Pretty sure."

He put on his windbreaker and zipped it up.

"Nice and warm?" Alison asked.

"Yeah."

"I'm freezing."

"You'd better go inside."

"Not yet." She took his hand and placed it on her naked breast. "That's better."

"Yeah."

She held his hand there and whispered, "I had a great time tonight, Mark."

"You *did*?"

"Well . . . it had its ups and downs."

"Jeez."

She laughed softly, winced, then stared through the darkness at him. "It *was* great."

He felt goose bumps crawl up his body, but wasn't sure why.

"We'll have to do it again sometime," she said.

"You mean . . . ?"

"Go out together. You know." She pressed his hand more tightly against her breast. "You want to, don't you?"

"My God. Sure I do. Of course."

"Me, too."

Then Mark laughed softly and whispered, "No conditions next time, right?"

"Only one."

141

The Wilds

This tale is dedicated to Algernon Blackwood
with special thanks for "The Willows" and
"The Wendigo"

June 16

I guess I'm all set to go. First thing in the morning, it's off to the wilds.

Fun and games.

I don't know why I'm doing it. To get over Cora, maybe. Or maybe it's just to torture myself. Who ever knows about this stuff anyway? The thing is, we had it planned for a month. The day after finals, we'd drive to Lost River Wilderness Area and spend five days backpacking. Just the two of us.

It was all planned.

It was about the only thing we talked about, how cool it would be. We mapped the trip, planned the menu, bought camping gear and supplies. We even got okays from our parents. I don't know what she told hers, but I let mine think I'd be going off to the boonies with a couple of guys from the dorm.

If they'd known I was going with a girl, they

would've shit. Probably. They've got this thing about me finishing college. They seem to think if I get really serious about a girl, I'll end up marrying her, dropping out of school and turning into a wino. They would've considered a campout with a girl *very* serious.

Anyway, they don't have to worry about me and Cora.

The bitch. Fuck her.

I'm going anyway. I'm going without her. Why not? Who needs her? Thoreau says, "I've found few companions so companionable as solitude." Something like that. And he was right. You start getting really close to someone, and the next thing you know you get the dump.

Well, you can't dump yourself.

It's not that I WANT to go alone.

I want HER to go with me. Oh, God, it would've been so great.

Shit. This isn't supposed to be a goddamn whiny sob-sister diary. So cut it out. This is the journal of my great adventure—Ned Champion, Pathfinder, Frontier Scout, Mountain Man.

June 17

I slept in. Even after I woke up, I had a hard time *getting* up. It was like, with Cora gone, there wasn't any good reason to do anything.

Pretty dumb. I literally didn't know she existed until last September when school started. We never talked till we ended up sitting next to each other in French—and that was after the winter break. It was March before we ever *did* anything together. So, basically, when it comes right down to it, I was going along just fine without her all my life until four months ago. Pretty damn stupid to get so crazy about losing her to that cocksucking piece of shit Whitworth, considering how I used to be just fine without her.

Hope they both rot and drop dead.

(There I go again. Oh well. Guess I can write whatever I damn well want. Who's going to stop me? I'd just better make sure this thing never falls into the wrong hands.)

Anyway, I didn't want to get up this morning so I stayed in bed thinking about Cora and how she wasn't really that big a deal. We'd had a fling for a few months. So what? Plenty of fish in the sea. (That's what Dad used to always tell me after I broke up with someone. It helped a lot. What a crock.) But the thing is, I told myself that Cora hadn't been the right girl for me. Obviously, ha ha. Otherwise, she wouldn't have— anyway, the RIGHT GIRL must be still up ahead for me. Waiting somewhere in the future. Maybe even today.

So I finally got going. Better late than never.

The place here is called "Randy's." I don't know

whether Randy is the name of the owner or how the waitress makes you feel. Right after I finished my bacon cheeseburger and started catching up with this stuff, she stopped behind me so close that her hip pushed against my shoulder. She wore this very short skirt. She felt hot, and made me hot—hot both ways, embarrassed and horny. I shut the notebook real fast, probably too quick for her to read anything. "Whatcha up-to, honey?" she asked. "You an author?"

"I'm just keeping track of my travels," I told her.

"Gonna put me in there?" Her hip gave me a soft bump.

I looked up at her. What I saw was mostly boob, but her face was up above it, grinning down at me. "Sure. You'll be in it." That seemed to please her, so she mussed my hair for me. Then she went away. It kind of choked me up, the way she'd mussed my hair. I don't know why. I think it made me feel kind of lonely.

Her name is Donna, by the way. It's on her name tag, is how I know. Donna. It's such a soft, sweet name. It makes me think of marshmallows.

Anyway, I'd better finish this off and get going. I'll leave Donna an extra big tip.

I made it. Took longer than I thought, though. I stopped for supper at a really neat place in the boonies. It had gas pumps out front. Inside, it had everything. It was part general store, part bait shop, and had a lunch counter at one end where I ate a cheeseburger and fries. A lot of interesting people were there, including a couple of cute gals, but nobody talked to me so there isn't much to report.

I got here after sundown. At dusk.

By here I mean the end of the line. It's a roadhead in the middle of nowhere. Cora and I had found it on our map of the Lost River area. It's as far as you can go by car. Our plan was to park here and start hiking.

To get here, I had to spend at least an hour on a dirt road that wasn't any wider than my car. Bushes kept scraping the sides. This roadhead is nothing more than a wide place where the road comes to a stop.

Mine is the only car here.

Funny, but I kept on thinking how maybe there would be one other car—Cora's yellow VW bug. When I drive in, she leaps out and runs to me. We run to each other and hug, both of us crying because we're so happy about being together again.

It's funny the stuff you think after you've broken up with someone like that.

Anyway, she didn't come. Nobody is here except me.

It's kind of spooky.

I haven't even stepped out of the car since I got here. But there's no reason to step out, anyway.

Since I've arrived so late, my plan is to spend the night in the car. Why bother taking everything out and setting up camp? This way, I'll save a lot of unpacking and stuff. I'll be more comfortable, too. And safer, ha ha.

It's been getting darker. Right now, all the trees and bushes look like different shades of gray. Nothing outside has much color. It's like a black-and-white movie. And the black is everywhere, just beyond where the trees start. You can't help wondering if somebody is out there, watching you.

It's more than just wondering. You *feel* like someone's spying on you. Someone wild and predatory.

Great. I'm going to scare myself if I don't watch out. I just now had to turn on the "courtesy light." Now I can see what I'm writing again.

The doors are locked. Though a lot of good that would do if anyone wanted to get at me.

I can always drive away if there's trouble. I've kept the key in the ignition, just in case.

Probably, nobody *is* out there. The old imagination is doing this to me, cooking up boogeymen.

It's all because I've never gone out like this alone before. I've always camped with Mom, Dad, Bob, the Boy Scouts, or buddies. Never alone. It's being alone that's giving me such a bad case of the creeps.

Nobody is out there—for sure not some kind

of slobbering Wildman eager to gnaw my bones. It's stupid.

Probably nobody within miles except for me.

June 18

It's morning. What a night! I had to quit writing before I was done. I just couldn't stand sitting in the car with the *light* on. I felt like I was in a display window. Talk about getting a case of the creeps!

I'm some outdoorsman, all right.

Once the light was out, I spent about an hour staring into the dark. It got so I thought I could see people sneaking around, peeking out from behind tree trunks, rushing from one tree to another.

I climbed into the backseat. Did it like a kid, crawling over the top of the front seat. I did it that way so I wouldn't have to get out of the car. Then I stretched out and tried to sleep. I shut my eyes. I tried to think pleasant thoughts. Cora sure didn't qualify. Thinking about her only got me upset.

So I thought about Donna, instead. The way she looked in her fresh white waitress uniform. The way her hip felt pushing against me. I made up a story in my head about how she wanted me to meet her in the parking lot at the end of her shift. The story didn't go very far, though. I must've fallen asleep pretty fast.

All of a sudden, I was wide awake and scared. The way I was stretched out along the backseat, the only window in sight was the one above my feet. Moonlight was shining through it.

I couldn't take my eyes off it. Any second, some kind of horrible face would press against the glass. I must've stared at that damn window for an hour.

Had a thoroughly wonderful time.

While that hour was going on, I decided to drive back to civilization first thing in the morning. Screw the camping trip.

Anyway, I finally figured that the locked doors would probably keep out the boogeyman long enough for me to scurry back into the driver's seat and get the hell away. That calmed me down. I almost fell asleep again. But then I had to take a leak.

It wasn't a necessity yet. But the urge was there. Once you know you've gotta go, there's no way to fall asleep till you've taken care of it. All you can do is lay there and think about it and feel it getting worse and worse.

It shouldn't have been a problem. I've normally got no qualms about peeing outside, just as long as there's some privacy. But it *was* a problem. A major problem. If I stepped outside the car, somebody might jump me.

Totally irrational. But I was totally scared.

I lay there for the longest time, my problem growing worse, and tried to figure out a solution. One thing was impossible—holding it till sunup. I searched for a container. Nothing. In with my camping gear were things that might've been used: water bottle, tin cup, mess kit, hiking boots, and so on. But all that stuff was locked in the trunk. So I couldn't get to them without leaving the car.

On my feet were Nikes of porous fabric, which would leak all over the place.

For a while, I considered climbing into the front seat and driving off. But what would that accomplish? A change of location, that's all. I wouldn't be able to hold it long enough to reach civilization.

So it came to a choice. Do it inside the car and smell the place up, or not.

For a while, I toyed with the idea of shooting it out an open window. Not being able to stand up, though, how would I go about that? There might be a way to position myself at an open window, but it would be awkward. It would require being snug against the opening (if I wanted to miss the car) with my dick outside my pants. What if somebody reached up and grabbed it?

Another possibility was to kneel on my seat, ease the door open just a bit, and aim through the gap. Better by far than hanging it out a window. But hardly safe.

Not being able to *see* alongside the car—or underneath it—I just couldn't help but worry that some horrible person might be hiding, waiting to grab me.

While all these things ran through my head, my condition got wore and worse. Time was running out. Something had to be done soon, or it would be too late.

Nobody's out there, I kept telling myself. It's all in your head. You're nothing but a little kid afraid of the dark.

A yella-belly.

I've been called yellow a lot, ever since I was a really little kid. But I had a higher opinion of myself. I wasn't yellow, just smart. Prudent. Too bright to do something stupid and reckless.

But sitting in the car last night, gritting my teeth and trying not to pee my jeans, I knew I *was* yellow. I'd always been yellow and I was still yellow.

And then I decided to stop being yellow.

A line from *Julius Caesar* kept going through my head. It's one of my favorites. "Danger knows full well that I am more dangerous than he." I kept thinking that over and over again.

It's a little weird what happened next.

I was a little crazy, I guess.

It seemed to me that if "Danger" got the idea that I really was "more dangerous than he," then maybe I'd be safe. Like a Wildman might be afraid to attack a wilder man.

Something like that probably only makes sense when you're scared out of your mind.

Anyway, I actually *felt* pretty wild as I stripped off my clothes and sprang out the door. Yelling and waving my knife overhead, I ran around the car. After the first trip around, I knew that nobody was lurking there. But I didn't stop. I dashed around the car again and again and again. To make it look good, maybe. To make it look like I was really a dangerous lunatic.

Then I dashed straight into the middle of the parking area, where the moonlight was. I stopped in the milky glow, spread my feet wide, arched my back, thrust both arms high and did a pretty good Tarzan call. And answered nature's call.

I didn't feel a bit scared.

I didn't feel a bit cold, either, even though a chilly wind was blowing and I didn't have on a stitch of clothes except for my shoes.

All I felt was free and wild and excited.

Between that excitement and how bad I'd needed to go, I probably set some kind of new distance record.

I felt *really* good.

I spent a while outside the car, but then started

to worry that a ranger might come along and see me. That's a laugh. What had happened to being scared to death of wild forest boogeymen?

Anyway, I got dressed and stretched myself out on the backseat and fell asleep right away.

This morning, I built a fire and made coffee. I ate some dried fruit and nuts. I've been drinking good, hot coffee while working on my journal.

I changed my mind about driving off. Obviously. Somehow, last night, I conquered my fears of being alone in a place like this.

I can hardly wait now to get started on my long hike into the depths of the wilds.

A hard uphill slog. My Christ. Switchbacks. And not a tree around for shade. I'm sweating like crazy. Thought I'd stop to rest for a few minutes, catch my breath, write a little.

I'm almost to the top. I think. I hope.

Anyway, a fabulous view from up here. Gray, craggy peaks off in the distance. Snow on plenty of them. The valley where I started out is way down there. It's so thick with forest that I can't even see the stream where I filled my water bottle and washed up this morning. I can't see my car, either, but a trace of the dirt road is visible. Not much wider than a hair.

A while ago, I met some people on their way down. They stopped and talked. A married couple, both pushing thirty I bet, but good-looking.

Both of them tanned and rugged. Wore matching costumes that made them look like they were on an African safari. But they wore cowboy hats, not pith helmets. They told me about a lake just below the pass, and how it has some decent campsites. They hadn't stayed there, but they'd stopped by the lake for a rest. "I went in for a dip," the woman said. "It was quite refreshing." Quite. She sounded and looked like a snob. They both did, for that matter.

I wonder what she wore when she took that dip of hers. If anything. Wish I could've been there to watch. She looked damn good in her safari outfit, probably looked a lot better out of it.

Ah, yes. I'm starting to feel better already.

Time to move on. Hope I don't drop dead of heat and exhaustion before I get to the top of this damn trail.

Yes yes yes! I made it—God knows how—to the top of the switchbacks. Very windy up there. It's sort of a pass between a couple of major-league peaks. I kept going until I found the lake. It was about half a mile beyond the ridge, a little bit lower, in a small valley all its own with trees along one side and nothing on the other side except for barren mountainside.

Nobody is here but me.

I'm staying. I've dumped my stuff at a campsite that has a fire circle with logs around it, and some sheltered, flat areas where people have probably pitched tents from time to time.

I got out of my hot sweaty clothes. Right now, it's a little past three in the afternoon. I'm in my swimming trunks and Nikes, sitting on a shelf of granite on the shore of the lake. I've got my pen and notebook, my water bottle, a good thick chocolate bar and a couple of trail cookies. The chocolate and cookies are designed for campers. They're so hard you can hardly bite into them. You feel like you might break your teeth. Good stuff, though. Scrum-bunctious!

The sun feels warm, but not too hot. There is a mild breeze that smells like Christmas trees. It also smells clean and brisk, making me think of snow. It blows softly against my bare skin.

The lake is clear blue. It sparkles with sunlight. Its surface is rippled a little by the breeze, and I can hear quiet hushed sounds as the water licks the rock in front of me.

I can also hear seagulls squealing. A few of them are coasting over the lake, gray or white against the blue of the cloudless sky. It amazes me that there are gulls at these high alpine lakes.

Getting here was hard. Torture. My legs still tremble and my shoulders ache. It was worth everything, though, to be here in this beauty and solitude.

This is the sort of place that makes you feel that every moment spent somewhere else was wasted.

Whatever Cora might be doing right now, it's lousy compared to this.

Tough luck, Cora.

If only she were her beside me, though. This would've been such a perfect place for making love. Especially for our first time. Now we'll probably never . . . Good going, now I'm depressed.

It's after supper. Ate a beef stew that came in a plastic pouch. Just had to add water, heat and serve. Vanilla pudding for dessert. I'm sitting by the fire, now. Nothing much happened since my last entry.

I kept expecting other hikers to show up and camp by the lake. Nobody did, though. I'm the only person here. This doesn't frighten me, which is funny. I think something must've happened to me last night when I did my "wildman" routine. Maybe it put me a little bit more in tune with nature. Who knows?

For whatever reason, I really like being out here alone in the wilderness. I'm glad nobody has stopped by the lake. It's all mine.

Whew! Just got back. Hiked all the way around the lake.

I took my flashlight along. After a while, its beam seemed like an intrusion. Got between me and the night. So I shut it off and walked by moonlight.

The moon made a silver path on the water, a path that led straight toward me and moved with me like the eyes in certain portraits.

At the other side of the lake I sat on a boulder and looked across at my campfire. Though it burned low, it gave off a lot of light. The ruddy glow even shimmered on the front of my tent, which must've been twenty feet from the fire. I could see the entire campsite clearly.

It was like looking at a theater stage. Watching it from a back row of seats, waiting for a player to walk on.

The player is here now, seated on a log by the fire, hunched over his writing pad.

But the spectator isn't across the lake to watch.

I'm a one-man show with only myself for an audience.

Huh?

Anyway, it was petty shocking to realize how the fire made my presence at the lake so conspicuous. The fire was like a sign that nature had been invaded by an alien.

I'm no invader. I want to be part of all this.

Anyway, now I'm going to douse the fire.

June 19

The tent was too—I don't know—confining, restricting? Just call me Nature Boy. On my other camping trips, I always slept in a tent. The tent was shelter from the weather, protection from bugs and other critters, and very much a hiding place. It enclosed me, concealed me, made me feel safe.

Those were always the good things about a tent. But they don't seem good anymore.

Last night, I couldn't stand being inside my tent. Pretty soon I dragged my sleeping bag outside. It was wonderful. I stayed awake for a long time, savoring the night, and woke up before sunrise when the air was still gray. There was dew on my sleeping bag, and on my face. It made my face feel sticky. My breath came out in white puffs.

I'd slept in my sweatsuit, which has a hooded top. It wasn't nearly enough to keep me warm after I was out of my sleeping bag. I shook like crazy. When I peed, my urine steamed.

I got the fire going again. It crackled and blazed and I crouched close to its heat. This morning, I *loved* my fire. And I *really* loved the sun when it finally rose high enough to clear the surrounding peaks.

In the movies, direct sunlight burns vampires—causes them terrible agony and pretty soon chars them down to a pile of ashes. The way the sunlight felt this morning reminded me of that. Because to me it was the exact opposite. I craved it. I felt like a starving man presented with a feast. It *restored* me.

I took off my sweats so I could feel the sun all

over. The sun's heat and the cool fresh morning breeze. It felt awfully good. It got me excited, too. I had this urge to circle the whole lake like I did last night, only do it naked. I didn't have the nerve, though. Somebody might come along the trail and see me. With that in mind, I only stayed naked long enough to bring my jeans out of the tent and put them on.

So I'm not quite the Nature Boy I'd like to be.

What the hell, I'm new at this.

Also, this area is too well traveled. It might seem like I have the whole place to myself, but there could be hikers just around a bend in the trail.

I need to go deeper into the wilds.

Today's hiking has been a lot easier than yesterday. For one thing, the trail has been up and down instead of a steady, steep climb. For another, my pack is much lighter. I left the tent behind.

Took it down after breakfast, rolled it, and hid it among the rocks near the lake shore. I'll retrieve it on the way out.

Now, of course, there'll probably be thunderstorms.

Who cares? I'm well rid of the tent.

Today, I ran into several groups of campers. Maybe twenty people, in all. Sure is a change from yesterday. And not a change I welcomed, either.

The problem was, quite a few trails converged in the area beyond my lake.

Even though I wanted to be alone, I acted friendly. I had nice chats with just about everyone. The basics were always the same. How long have you been out? Where did you spend last night? Where are you heading, and by which route? If somebody was coming from where you were going, you wanted to find out how the trail was and where there might be a good place to camp. I paid close attention to everybody's routes because I wanted to spend the night without company.

One more thing about the basics of trail-side conversation. Nobody could resist commenting about the fact that I was out here alone. I got all kinds of reactions. Some people gave me funny looks and soon hurried off. Others were simply curious. Some admired my bravery. A few seemed envious—as if they would much rather be out here by themselves than stuck with a group of annoying friends or relatives. What I got most often, though, were remarks like this:

"You must be nuts. What if you break a leg? Who goes for help?"

And, "You're going smack up against the first rule of wilderness survival, boy."

And, "You'd better stay healthy, that's all I've got to say."

Four guys from U.C. Berkeley actually invited

me to join their group. I declined. Threw my Thoreau "solitude" quote at them, which seemed to impress one guy, but made two of them smirk. The fourth member of their party actually said, "What a dork."

Quite a few women crossed my path today. I enjoyed looking. Some were stout, some slender. Some were fairly pretty while others looked ordinary or worse. But I saw plenty of bare, tanned legs, shorts packed with firm buttocks, and midriffs on a couple of gals who wore their shirts pulled up and tied. The best thing I saw all day was a blonde in a tank top. She wasn't much in the face department, but her shirt was almost transparent and she didn't wear anything under it.

She was the high point of my day, so far.

Around midafternoon, I came to a nice lake. Unfortunately, people had already arrived and had their tents set up. So I kept going. The next lake also had a group of campers. From my map, I could see that there wasn't another lake within five miles. No way would I make it that far today. But I kept hiking and things worked out.

A stream cut across the trail. It was bridged by an old, fallen tree. Instead of crossing, I made my way upstream and found a good place to spend the night. A good, *secluded* place.

The trail is far below, blocked from sight by boulders and trees.

It bothers me a little that I've done this—taken

a detour away from the trail in order to find a private place to spend the night. It makes me feel furtive, like I'm hiding out.

I just wish all the other people would disappear so I could have the mountains completely to myself.

Maybe if I go farther. Deeper in.

The problem is, I only brought food for ten days, so I have to begin heading back after the fifth. Which only gives me two more days.

Right now, I don't feel like I want to return so soon.

That could change, though. If it continues to be like Grand Central Station around here, I might be glad to leave.

My place here, at least, is private. It's great. The first thing I did was strip and wade into the water. The stream is so cold it hurts. I couldn't stand it for very long. But I found a pothole in the rocks. It held warm water that must've come from a rainstorm. Luckily, it wasn't very stagnant yet. It felt great. I stayed in it for a long time. It probably wasn't all that fresh and clean, though, so after getting out, I rinsed in the cold stream.

I'm warm again, now. I've been sitting in the sunlight writing all this for about an hour. Probably got myself a great sunburn. But maybe not. Maybe it's too late in the day for sunburns.

Better quit writing, now. Things to do before dark.

June 20

I cooked supper in the early evening yesterday, then doused my fire and sat by the stream to eat. Had mosquito trouble at around sundown when I was cleaning my mess kit and stuff. Had to get dressed, and also stink myself up with repellent. When the wind kicked up, the mosquitoes disappeared.

Turned in early. Slept great. I must've really been bushed, because I hardly even noticed the solid rock under my sleeping bag and foam pad. Not even the noise of the rushing water bothered me. It was loud, too. From the sound of the stream, you'd think I had spread my sleeping bag in the middle of a freeway.

I woke up this morning feeling an awful urgency to get moving. Only two days, then I'd need to head back. I didn't even build a fire and have coffee, just packed and hit the trail as fast as I could.

It's noon, now. I've finally stopped to rest and eat and catch up with the journal.

Made very good time. And the number of intruders has dwindled since yesterday. Thank God. I'm obviously making some progress.

Something funny is going on. It's not really so funny, though. I don't know exactly why, but I'm feeling more and more reluctant to encounter other people.

This morning when hikers approached on the trail, I felt apprehensive. I greeted them, smiling, but didn't stop to chat. My main concern was to get away from them. The thing is, there was nothing wrong with these people. They seemed perfectly nice and ordinary.

About an hour after my lunch break this afternoon, I heard more people coming. They were still out of sight beyond a bend in the trail, but I could hear them.

So I hid.

I hurried off the trail and climbed up into the rocks and crouched out of sight.

At the time, I told myself it was just a simple matter of preferring my own company. Sort of like turning down a party invitation because you'd rather stay home and read a book.

While I crouched there hiding, though, I started to feel scared. Scared that the strangers coming along the trail would *find* me. My mouth went dry. My heart thudded. I trembled all over. It was ridiculous. They had no reason to hunt for me. If I hadn't fled, we would've met on the trail, smiled and chatted. No big deal.

After they'd passed my hiding place, a change came over me. Something seemed to *grow* out of my fear.

Excitement.

They hadn't seen me, didn't have a clue that I'd been crouched only a few yards away. I was invisible.

An invisible man.

Feeling exhilarated, I returned to the trail. I laughed quite a lot. Felt downright gleeful.

It changes everything, being invisible.

Later on this afternoon, I heard another batch of people coming. I bounded off the trail, climbed the slope and hid among the rocks. Just like last time. But very different, too. This time, I didn't simply cower in hiding until the strangers had gone by; I raised my head and peered down at them.

Spied on them.

A man was in the lead, followed by a woman. This was an uphill grade, so they took their time. They trudged, leaning forward against the weight of their packs, their heads down. The yellow dust kicked up by the man swirled around the boots and shins of the woman. She wore red shorts and a gray T-shirt. She was built. The backpack straps pulling at her shoulders made her breasts really stick out. I could tell by how they moved that she was wearing a bra. The sight of them stirred me up a lot, anyway.

Basically, I was looking at nothing I wouldn't have seen if I'd stayed on the trail and said "howdy." God only knows why it should make such a difference, watching it in secret. But it does. It sure does.

I thought about following the couple. I *wanted* to. But the gal wasn't all that special anyway, and they were heading in the wrong direction.

That's about all for now. It's midafternoon and I hope to reach Mascot Lake in time to make camp before dark. Sure hope nobody else has the same idea.

After catching up with the writing, I returned to the trail and continued my journey.

Arrived at Mascot Lake about an hour later. It was some distance from the main trail, so my view took in the entire lake. It looked blue and cold and wonderful. A thick crescent of woods along the near side would provide welcome shade, plus shelter from the winds. It looked like a very fine place to camp.

Best of all, it looked deserted.

I was overjoyed at the prospect of having the lake to myself. But then I noticed the tent. A green tent, nearly invisible among the trees and shadows near the shore.

With a curse, I kicked a stone. The stone went skipping over the trail, raising puffs of yellow dust.

What the hell, I thought. Win a few, lose a few.

I kept walking. From off toward the lake came quiet sounds of voices, the chunking of a hatchet.

One of the voices most definitely belonged to a woman. Staying on the trail, still walking, I scanned the area near the tent and spotted two figures. One was bent over and seemed to be cutting wood for the campfire. The other watched. It was impossible to tell which was the woman because they were too far away, standing among trees that partly blocked my view, and covered by the gloom of shadows.

I kept walking.

But the earlier thrill of hiding and spying on the hikers was mild compared to the fever that grabbed me as I walked away from Mascot Lake.

I could return as the invisible man!

Yes!

After "disappearing" myself around a bend, I left the trail and made my way back toward the lake. Found a good, hidden place surrounded by walls of rock. This will be my base camp. I've gotten out of my sweaty clothes, and eaten a meal of jerky and gorp and dried peaches.

The notion of sneaking up on the campers really has me excited. I can hardly stand it.

Did Apaches feel this way just before they crept up on unwary settlers?

I'm nervous enough without trying it naked. So I've gotten into my trunks and Nikes. Now I'm all caught up on the writing. Still a couple of hours before dark. I'm off!

June 21

After leaving here yesterday, I made my way back to Mascot Lake. Kept low, crawled. And finally positioned myself among some rocks directly across the lake from the camp. Like most alpine lakes, this one isn't very large. From where I hid, I could've thrown a rock as far as the tent.

Not until I had taken my position did I actually raise my head and study the campsite. It had a low, round wall of rocks for a fireplace, and enough wood piled nearby to last all night. There were sawed-off logs here and there for seats. A red backpack was propped upright against one of the logs. A blue backpack was propped against the foot of a tree. The tent was a few yards behind the fireplace, its front facing the lake. The flaps were down so I couldn't see inside.

I was giving the place a good inspection when a motion off to the side caught my eye.

A woman in the trees. And she had a lot of bare skin.

My heart whammed.

But the thrill faded as soon as I got a better look at her. She was about twenty years old, had brown hair styled like a football helmet, a flat face with a wide nose, and a short, stocky body. She didn't look flabby, just broad. She wore a black bikini that would've looked better on someone tall and slim. On her, it looked peculiar. She did have a good tan, though. It was her best feature.

She seemed to be amusing herself by throwing the hatchet at a tree off to the right of the tent. On the first try I witnessed, she planted the hatchet into the trunk. She strode forward and pulled it out, then turned around and seemed to measure her strides.

I watched her for a while.

Felt like throwing something at *her*. I'd gotten myself all in a sweat to spy on this gal, and worked my tail off sneaking around to where I might have a good view, only to find out she was a bow-wow. Shit!

I was ready to leave, but didn't dare.

Where was the guy?

Until I found him, I couldn't move; he might be in a position to spot me.

I scanned the entire stretch of trees over there, the whole shoreline, the rocky slopes curving around my side of the lake.

Every ounce of thrill and excitement had drained out of this little adventure. I'd turned into a Peeping Tom for *this*, and now I was going to be caught and probably beaten half to death or something by this gal's boyfriend/lover/what-ever.

The gal herself might end up using her hatchet on me.

They could tie me to her target tree, and have some sport.

I remembered my sheath knife. Still on the belt of my jeans, back with the rest of my stuff. The idea that I might need to defend myself had never occurred to me.

Maybe I would be able to outrun the guy.

WHERE WAS HE???

Near panic, I looked everywhere. Still no sign of him.

Had he gone for a stroll up the trail? Maybe he was taking a snooze inside the tent.

Maybe I'd better try to get while the getting was good.

But I couldn't move. I felt frozen. Frozen, but burning up. Even this late in the afternoon, the sun was bearing down on me. There seemed to be no breeze at all. I was being broiled, and sweat poured off me. Still, frozen is what I was.

I *had* to know where the guy was.

Then the tent flaps bulged, spread apart, and out came the girl's companion.

A brunette with rich, gleaming hair. Tresses swung in front of her face as she crawled from the tent and stood up. Then she swept them aside. Though her face was a little indistinct because of the distance, what I could see of it looked very good. She actually seemed beautiful. Dark skin, stark white eyes and teeth.

Standing in front of the tent, she stretched as if she might've just awakened. Yawned, went to tip-toes, arched her back, reached her arms up high, twisted her body slowly from side to side.

She wore a white, string bikini.

She was tall and slender, tawny. Long-limbed and sleek. She looked like the sort of elegant fashion model who usually has breasts the size of tea cups. But hers were about three times that size. They looked like twin loaves held loosely by the pouches of her bikini top. Between their smooth, rounded sides was a shadowed valley.

Anyway, they were terrific.

She was terrific.

After finishing her stretch, she turned away from the tent and walked toward her friend. She had a great walk. Her buttocks took turns flexing. Between them was a white thong.

I heard voices as she stepped close to her friend, but I couldn't make out the words.

Then she started throwing the hatchet.

God, what a sight!

She threw nine or ten times at the tree. Each time she planted the hatchet into the trunk, her friend clapped. The couple of occasions she missed, they both laughed. The other gal would run to fetch the hatchet, and bring it back to her.

Then that one took a few turns.

After a while, they quit. The small one whacked the hatchet into a stump near the fireplace. Side by side, they walked toward the lake. And straight toward me.

They waded gingerly into the water, carrying on a lot about how cold it was. They shuddered and squealed. They acted as if they were being tortured and found it hilarious.

In with all the cries about the freezing water, and how they were dying and so on, they shouted each other's names a few times. The fabulous one was Gloria. Her dumpy friend was Susie.

As Gloria stepped carefully into deeper water, Susie splashed her from behind. Gloria shrieked and flinched rigid as if she'd been jabbed in the back with a cattle prod. Her breasts did a jump of their own. One hopped right out of her bikini and swung through the air as she whirled around. It was shiny in the sunlight. It was very white where it had no tan. The nipple was dark and stuck way out. "Now you've done it!" she shouted. She chased Susie through the shallow part of the lake, giggling and gasping, ducking low every now and then to fling water.

They were both drenched by the time they faced off for the showdown. Standing a couple of yards apart in knee-deep water, they bent over and slapped at the surface like crazy, flinging frothy torrents at each other.

Susie suddenly caught a mouthful and choked. She turned away, coughing. Immediately, Gloria quit splashing.

"Are you okay?"

Susie kept coughing.

Gloria slapped her on the back a few times. Her hand made loud smacking sounds against the wet skin. She had a worried look on her face.

"Are you okay?"

Susie's head bobbed. She coughed a few more times, then took deep breaths.

Gloria patted her back more gently. "You okay now?"

"Yeah. Just . . . choked on some water." Susie bent down and held her knees.

Gloria took the opportunity to fool with her bikini top and tuck her breast into its pouch. Smiling, she asked, "Want to race?"

Susie straightened up. She turned around. "I don't think so."

"Come on. I'll give you a headstart."

A corner of Susie's mouth turned up. "You'll give *me* a headstart?"

"It's only fair. I almost drowned you."

"I'm fine. I don't need any headstart. You're the one who needs a headstart, honey."

Gloria smiled. "If you insist. Where to?"

They checked around, then Susie nodded toward the far end of the lake. "See that flat rock sticking out?" The lake was not very wide, but fairly long. The flat rock appeared to be at least fifty yards away.

"Maybe we should swim *that* way," Gloria said, and pointed behind her.

Susie turned to look.

And that's when Gloria dived in the opposite direction. She came up swimming hard for the flat rock that Susie had suggested as their goal.

A moment later, Susie hit the water.

Gloria already had a lead of about one body-length.

I didn't stick around to see who won.

With both of them swimming off like that, I had a great chance to make a clean escape. So I took it. Scampered over the rocks and got away from the lake and ran.

By the time I got back here, I was worn out. Drained. Exhausted. Too much excitement.

I turned in early. For a long time, though, I couldn't fall asleep. I lay there cozy in my sleeping bag, my mind in a turmoil. Sometimes, I got all excited about Gloria. Other times, I got a sick feeling.

The sick feeling was probably guilt. My little visit to Mascot Lake had seemed at the time like a great adventure. A daring mission. Invisible man on the prowl, spying on babes.

When you come down to it, though, what I did was kind of perverted.

I finally made the decision to stay away from Gloria's camp. I would not, under any circumstances, pay another visit. Come morning, I told myself, I would hit the trail and raise dust.

That calmed me down. I fell asleep. Didn't sleep well, though. Too many vivid, wild dreams. They mostly featured Gloria, of course. They had me feverish and thrashing around. Some were wonderful, some horrible.

Finally, I woke up and saw that the sky was getting light. Not dawn yet, but near enough.

Awfully cold outside my bag. I shook like crazy, getting dressed and packing away my gear. But I was on my way in record time. The shivers stopped after I'd been on the trail for about five minutes.

Anyway, what I did yesterday was wrong, but I feel pretty good now. Kept my vow to leave without any more nonsense. Didn't cave in.

Hiked for a couple of hours, just to put a good distance between myself and temptation. No sign of anyone all morning. I'm determined, though, to act normal if people do come along. Not hide, not spy. No more "invisible man" stuff. Just stay on the trail and say hello and maybe have a nice chat.

I can see the trail from here. It's a distance off, but not out of sight. Maybe I'm trying to prove that I don't need to hide. Who knows?

The creek here is noisy. It rushes quick over the rocks, and sometimes it throws an icy splash against my back. Feels good, even though it makes me flinch.

After getting here, I built a fire. I'd missed my

morning coffee, not wanting to make a fire while I was still close to Mascot Lake. The girls might've been awake, might've seen the smoke.

So I treated myself to a lot of hot coffee, and also cooked a skillet full of bacon and eggs. Fake eggs, of course. But the meat was real, scraped from a "bacon bar" that is shaped like a cake of soap. It was a very fine breakfast.

Afterward, I killed the fire, changed into my trunks, and cleaned my cooking stuff at the stream. Also took the opportunity to wash up and brush my teeth. Pretty soon, everything was taken care of except this.

It's incredible the number of pages I've gotten done this morning. It's taken forever. My butt kept falling asleep from sitting on the rocks. One time, my dick even went numb. Had to stand up before the feeling would return.

A lot of work, but I'm caught up. My middle finger has a red dent from the pressure of the pen.

I like it here beside this creek. Today marks the midpoint of my trip. The fifth day since leaving the car. I haven't eaten as much food as planned, so I don't actually have to start heading back tomorrow. But I think I will. Five days out is far enough. In some ways, too far.

Instead of pushing on, I'll spend the night here. First thing in the morning, I'll start heading back for the car.

It'll be good to return to civilization.

They've stopped for lunch. I can see them from here if I peer over the edge of rock behind me. They're down below on the trail. Last time I looked, they'd taken off their packs and were perched on a boulder.

What happened is this.

I'd finished the writing and was feeling lazy, so I spread out my sleeping bag near the stream and stretched out on it. Very comfortable. Lying in the shade. Warm. A nice, soft breeze.

I was almost asleep when somebody laughed.

And there they were, hiking up the trail, Susie in front, Gloria following. I was shocked, to say the least. Always figured, for no good reason, that they were on their way in the *other* direction.

Anyway, they didn't seem to spot me. Just kept going.

I threw all my stuff together fast and went after them.

I've been following them ever since, staying a good safe distance to the rear, staying out of sight always. I'm sure they haven't seen me.

Just now I looked down to check on them. They're still sitting on the rock. Sharing a foil pouch of something—trail mix, gorp, nuts, who knows? Gloria had a plastic bottle in one hand. Red liquid inside. Kool-aid, maybe.

This is the nearest I've been to her. She's even more beautiful than I thought. God, what a knockout!!!

She's been wearing a big gray felt hat, but she took it off and tossed it onto her pack. She has a red bandanna tied around her neck. She's wearing a tan, short-sleeved shirt with epaulets and button-down pockets. It looks expensive, like a shirt from one of those mail order houses that specializes in outdoor stuff. It looks loose and comfortable. It isn't tucked in, and it's unbuttoned to about halfway down. Through the gap, I can see the sides of her breasts and the space between them. Her shorts match the shirt. They're sort of baggy. They'd probably reach to her knees, but she has them rolled up. She's wearing regular white crew socks and big leather hiking boots.

She almost looks like she's modeling the stuff, except that her hair is mashed down from the hat and she's sweaty and dusty.

Susie is wearing—who cares? Never mind.

Will sign off now, and keep an eye on things.

Got some time to kill. "You can't kill time without injuring eternity," so says Thoreau. But I can't go anywhere for a while.

Just ahead, things open up. That's the problem. The trail cuts across a very long stretch of barren slope. Nowhere for me to hide. If I start following and one of the girls looks back, I'll be spotted. Can't have that.

If there were some other hikers around, I might chance it. Haven't seen any all day, though. We must be somewhere pretty remote. With nobody else on the trail, I'd be too conspicuous. So I have to just wait until Gloria and Susie are out of sight.

Hope I don't lose them.

Might be better if I *do* lose them. Don't know what's wrong with me. I had left them behind. I was free from them. But this morning when they hiked by, it was like they threw a chain around me and dragged me after them.

Guess I'm nuts.

Nuts all right. Nuts about Gloria.

It's crazy, though. I don't even know her. In a way, I don't *want* to know her. (That sounds a little crazy, too.) The thing is, it's great to just observe her from afar like I've been doing. It would change everything if I actually talked to her. I'm sure of that. It would lessen her. She'd lose her magic.

I'd lose mine, too. Wouldn't be invisible anymore.

Maybe I've just stumbled onto the secret of a great relationship—don't have one. Ha ha.

I just looked. I can still see them. They'll be *awfully* far ahead by the time it's safe for me to follow. I'm tempted to start out after them now, but don't want to blow it.

They got such a good lead that I didn't see them again for a couple of hours. By then, they'd already pitched camp near the south end of Big Boy

Lake. I glimpsed their tent through the trees, then looked away quick in case they happened to be watching me.

Big Boy is much larger than Mascot. Like every other lake up here, it's in a basin surrounded by mountains. This one has a lot more trees than most, though. They are at both ends, and thick along the whole western shore.

I walked the length of Big Boy. From what I saw, it looked as if nobody was there except the girls.

Perfect.

Just them and me.

My plan was to camp at Little Boy. The map showed it just north of Big and at a slightly lower elevation. When I looked down at it, though, my plan changed. Little Boy looked like a nightmare—just a scoop of water surrounded by granite slopes. No more than five or six trees grew by its shore. I could see twice that many under the water, sprawled out white. A lake couldn't look any more desolate and creepy than Little Boy. They should've named it Little Dead Boy.

Where the trail dipped downward on its way toward that nasty place, I ducked behind a clump of boulders. I waited a while. Then I snuck over to Big Boy, staying low.

Found a good spot for the night. A small clearing surrounded by trees, bushes, and boulders. It's not far from shore. And it's almost at the opposite end of the lake from the girls' camp. Not much chance that they'll find out I'm here.

I didn't build a fire, of course. Made a meal of dried fruit, cookies, and chocolate. Will take along my bacon bar for later. And my water bottle.

I'm going now to see what they're up to. Keeping my clothes on, this time, though I've changed out of my hiking boots. Taking my jacket, too. It'll be dark soon, and I don't want to freeze.

June 22

Back to where I left off. Seems like a long, long time ago that I went looking for Gloria and Susie. Just yesterday afternoon, though.

God, I'm lucky to be back.

Somewhat the worse for wear, as they say. But back.

Anyway . . .

Yesterday afternoon, I made my way toward their camp very carefully. Silent, invisible. Took a long time. After every step, I stopped to listen. Finally heard their voices. I couldn't understand what was being said, but the voices told me where they were.

I found them between the front of their tent and the lake shore, Gloria sitting on a rock and reaching into her backpack while Susie knelt by the fireplace and busied herself breaking twigs in half.

They had both changed from hiking boots to sneakers. Otherwise, they were dressed the same as before.

I felt exposed, watching from behind a tree trunk. Searched for a better observation post, and found the perfect thing. Only a short distance from the rear of their tent was a boulder some fifteen or twenty feet high. It loomed like a tower over their campsite.

I made a big circle to avoid the girls, came in from behind, and climbed to the top. Not an easy climb by any means. That was good, though. The harder the climb, the less likely I was to have a visit from Gloria or Susie.

Great up there, almost like it was *meant* to be my lookout post. It was roughly round, about eight feet across, and had a sunken area in the middle. When I sat or knelt in the depression, it was like being inside a shallow bowl; I couldn't even begin to see the ground. Which meant I was well out of sight from down there.

This was almost too good to be true.

My own private world.

My only regret was that I hadn't brought my sleeping bag along. Or the rest of my stuff. This would've been a great place to make camp.

Right on top of them. So to speak.

From here, I would be able to watch them do *everything*. The sun hadn't gone down yet. In fact, it felt very hot. So they might go swimming. They might sunbathe. Or toss the hatchet around, like yesterday. Whatever, I'd have a bird's-eye view.

With my jacket to keep me warm, I should even be able to stay after dark, stick with them until they turned in. Once they were inside their tent for the night, I could climb down and return to my camp. Get some sleep. Come back before dawn and be ready atop my lookout by the time they got up. Their morning activities were sure to make a great show.

Oh, I had big plans.

On my belly, I squirmed toward the front of my rocky lookout. I peered over the edge just as Susie tipped her head to take a drink of water. Her eyes locked on mine.

Gave me a terrible sensation, like suddenly falling.

I ducked out of sight.

All my insides seemed to be cold, squeezed tight and shaking.

For a little while, the only sounds were the wind and some gulls. Maybe Susie hadn't seen me, after all.

Mistook my head for an owl? Thought I was a marmot, or something?

It's amazing the crap that runs through your

head. All you want is a way out. You want a Time Machine to travel you an hour backward so you can decide *not* to come here. You want to turn invisible for real, or at least be able to sink into the ground and disappear like a puddle of water. You want to take a flying leap and land on your feet and run like hell. *Anything*, just so you don't have to face the music.

Maybe it's for the best, I finally told myself. After all, I'd been starting to go off the deep end. Maybe getting caught is just what I needed.

Those are just a few of the things that zapped through my mind while I shivered and waited for the girls to react.

The wait seemed to last about five years. It was probably more like a minute. Then Susie called, "Who's up there? I saw you." She sounded very nervous. "There's no use hiding. Who are you? What are you doing up there?"

If I keep my mouth shut and don't show myself, they'll think I got away.

"Come on, mister." This time, it was Gloria's voice. It didn't sound nervous at all. Calm and patient. "We know you're up there. We can't just go on about our business and pretend you're not there, you know? We're out in the middle of nowhere and we've suddenly got a stranger lurking around. Hey, maybe you're a nice guy. Or maybe you're some kind of lunatic. The thing is, we can't just assume you're okay. So come on down and talk to us."

I thought about it. How could I convince them that I wasn't a threat, that I was indeed a nice guy, that they had nothing to fear from me?

"I've got a gun, mister," Gloria called.

Wonderful news. It almost made me fill my pants.

"If you don't come down on your own, I might have to use it on you."

She fired. Into the air, probably.

I crapped and peed simultaneously.

"Okay!" I yelled. "I'll come down. Just a minute." Real fast, I shucked off my shoes and jeans. My jockeys had caught the load. Got rid of them, and used my shirt to wipe. While I worked at it, I tried to talk my way out of things. "It's a free country, you know. I was here first. It's not my fault you decided to camp right where I already was."

"If you were here," Susie called, "you should've told us."

"I was scared. I don't know you two people. Maybe you're nice women. Or maybe you're a couple of lunatics."

"Very funny, mister," Gloria said. She didn't sound amused.

After hurrying into my jeans, I put my jacket on. "I mean it," I explained. "I was scared, so I decided to hide and look for a chance to sneak away."

"Stand up where we can see you," Gloria ordered.

Quickly, I slipped into my shoes. "You won't shoot, will you?"

"Just do what you're told."

I got to my feet and looked down over the edge. The girls were standing side by side near the front of their tent, both facing me, their heads back. Susie held the hatchet low by her hip. Gloria held a revolver, her arm up and bent at the elbow so that the gun was close to her ear. She had it pointed straight upward, not at me.

I raised my open hands, the way they do on TV.

"Is anybody else up there with you?" Gloria asked.

"No."

"Where're your friends?" Susie asked.

"I don't have any."

"Right. Nobody packs in alone."

"I did."

Susie glanced about as if she expected a sneak attack by my gang of pals. Then she looked up at me again. "Where are they?"

"There's nobody but me. Honest."

"Do you have some i.d.?" Gloria asked.

She was very good at saying things I didn't want to hear. Already, I had stopped being invisible. Once she took a look at my driver's license, I would stop being anonymous. God! She'd have my name, my parents' address!

Fortunately, the license was in my wallet, which I had left inside my backpack.

"I haven't got anything," I said.

"We'll see about that," Susie muttered.

"It's the truth. My parents won't let me get a driver's license until . . ."

"Shut up and come down here," Susie said.

"Okay." Nodding, I took a step backward.

Gloria's arm darted out. She aimed the revolver at me and shouted, "Stop! Come down the front."

Leaning forward, I peered down. And groaned. "I can't. I'll fall. It's too steep."

"I'm sorry about that," Gloria said. "Do it, anyway. I don't want you out of sight right now."

When you're trapped on top of a boulder, you don't have a lot of choices. You can't stay up there forever. They can either wait you out, climb up and get you, or find a higher place nearby where they can shoot down at you. (There were some trees within just a few yards of me.) So you've got to reach the ground, but you can't climb down fast enough to get away unshot. Also, you can't jump off the top without breaking yourself.

So I said, "Okay." With both girls watching, I started to make my way down the face of the boulder. It was awfully steep.

About halfway down, my foot slipped. I gasped and tried to hang on. Nothing to hang on *to*, though, so I fell backward. The ground knocked my legs out from under me, then smacked my butt. Then my back hit the dirt.

Gloria stuck the gun in my face. "Don't move."

That was a laugh.

Anyway, I just stayed sprawled on the ground,

gasping and trying to get my breath back. Susie crouched and searched me. My jacket was open. She flipped it open wider and ran her hands under it, feeling my bare sides from armpits to hips. She pulled the hunting knife out of the sheath on my belt. She patted my front pockets. She even checked my ankles.

While all that went on, Gloria stood about a yard beyond my head, leaning forward, her arm straight, the muzzle of her revolver no more than ten inches from my forehead. Looking at the hole gave me a funny ache—the weird kind of ache you get if you cross your eyes. So I didn't look at it much.

The way Gloria was bent over, her hair hung straight down past the sides of her face. Her face was upside-down, of course. She looked strange but beautiful.

Susie made me roll over. The ground was covered with pine needles. They were dry and prickly against my skin. She felt around under the back of my jacket, patted my seat pockets, ran her hands down my legs. "I guess he's okay," she said.

"Can I get up, now?" I asked.

"Don't move," Gloria said.

"What'll we do with him?"

"I'll just leave," I offered. "I'll get my gear and leave. Okay?"

"Not okay," Gloria said.

"I wasn't *doing* anything."

191

"Like hell you weren't," Susie said.

"We came out here," Gloria said, "to get away from people like you."

"People like me? What're you . . . ?"

"All the fucking perverts and rapists and murderers."

"I'm not . . ."

"You're *everywhere*, goddamn it! It used to be, you could at least go to the mountains and get away from all the degenerate scumbags."

"Even the mountains aren't safe," Susie added.

"They're safe!" I blurted. "I'm not anything! I'm just camping! You came along to where *I* was. I wasn't doing anything wrong. I promise. Please."

"Go over and get my rope," Gloria said.

Susie went for it, her footsteps crunching pine needles.

"What're you gonna do?" I asked. "Can't you just let me go?"

"So you can sneak up on us again?"

"I *didn't* sneak up on you."

Susie came back and stopped beside me. "What now?"

"Tie his hands behind his back."

Susie straddled me and tied my hands. After that was done, Gloria ordered me to stand up. Susie stayed behind me, holding the rope.

They got me into position, a tree branch several feet overhead. Then Susie tossed the rope over the branch. She caught the end. She pulled, hoisting my bound arms up behind me and forcing me up on tiptoes.

"Not that high," Gloria told her.

They made it so I could stand without getting my arms wrenched from their sockets. Then Susie tied the rope to the trunk.

"This is crazy," I said.

Susie smirked. "What're we supposed to do, let you go?"

"Yes!"

"You should just be glad we're reasonable, civilized people," Gloria said. "If we really wanted to play it smart, we'd incapacitate you."

"I *am* incapacitated!"

"You're *tied up*. There's a big difference. To you and to us. This is a lot more dangerous for us."

"Consider yourself lucky," Susie added.

They left me there, and started breaking camp. "What're you doing?" I asked.

"Getting out of here," Gloria said.

"Now?"

"Soon as we can."

"But it's almost dark."

"We're not gonna spend the night here, that's for sure."

"Why? Because of me?"

"What do *you* think?" Susie said.

"You don't have to go away."

"The hell we don't."

"What about me?"

"You're staying right where you are," Gloria said.

"Tied up?"

"You got it," Susie said.

"You'll be all right," Gloria told me. "I'm sure you'll manage to get loose sooner or later. When you do, don't come after us."

"Or you'll wish you hadn't," Susie said.

"You got off lucky this time."

About fifteen minutes later, they hefted their backpacks and hiked away.

It came as a relief to watch them leave.

Things could've gone so much worse. They'd had me at their mercy. They could've done *anything* to me—beaten me up, tortured me, killed me. Apparently, I had lucked out in going after a couple of gals with scruples about such things. They hadn't even taken my name, much less gotten their hands on my driver's license.

(I knew my license was safe because I watched them hike straight over to the trail and head north. They went nowhere near the place where I'd hidden my gear.)

Without knowing who I am, they can't do anything to me. Can't tell on me, get the law on me, or anything!

I got off lucky, all right. Nothing to show for being caught except a few bad scares, messing my pants, falling off a boulder and getting myself tied to a tree.

Could've been so damn much worse.

It actually did get worse around sundown. That's when the mosquitoes came. With my arms tied behind me, I couldn't do a thing about them. They flew underneath my open jacket. They settled on my face and neck and got in my ears.

But the mosquitoes made me so crazy that I finally escaped from the rope. I'd been working at the problem from the moment the gals left. I'd been taking it easy, though, turning my wrists inside their binding, sometimes tugging, twisting some more, gradually working the tightness out of the rope. I'd been making progress without hurting myself.

With the mosquitoes buzzing around me, landing on every exposed bit of skin, sucking my blood, making me itch all over, I went nuts and ripped my hands out of the rope. Took off layers of skin, but I didn't care.

Hands free, I slapped at the damn mosquitoes while I ran full speed to the lake. I paused long enough to strip, then ran into the water and dived.

The huge, soothing relief of ice cold water on mosquito bites is one of life's great pleasures.

I stayed in the lake for a long time. It was dark by the time I climbed out. Dark and very windy. No mosquitoes found me while I got dressed.

Back at the secluded place where I'd left my pack, I dug out a tube of ointment. Stripped again and hunted out all of my mosquito bites and dabbed them with goo. The ones I could reach, anyhow. I had bumps all over. Still do.

Anyway, the ointment helped some, but not much.

I climbed into my sleeping bag, feeling itchy and hot and miserable. Instead of counting sheep, I counted my mosquito bites. I tried to make up my mind which were the most itchy. It ended as a toss-up between the bites on my forehead and those on the backs of my fingers.

Finally, I got to sleep.

I woke up after sunup this morning. Searched around. No sign of the girls. Took another dip in the lake for the sake of my bites. Refreshed, I returned to camp and built a fire. Made my morning coffee, bacon and eggs. (Had to throw away the bacon bar I'd taken with me yesterday, as it had been in a front pocket of my jeans, gotten peed on, and later taken a dunk in the lake. But I had an extra in my pack.) After breakfast, dug out my journal here and found a nice private place in the rocks by the lake.

Have been taking my time, filling in all the details. Though I'm still itchy, it's eased off some. The sun feels very good. And so does the cool mountain breeze.

Nobody else has shown up here at Big Boy.

I wonder where Gloria and Susie are. Did they hike all night to get away from me?

I have to go back to their camp, now. See if I can find my knife, though Susie might've taken it with her.

Also, I left my water bottle on top of the boulder. I don't look forward to climbing up there again, but I need it.

Pretty scary, going back. I was afraid they'd show up and catch me again. I kept looking around, listening. What made it worse was realizing they really *might* show up.

Just suppose they started to worry about me? They were decent people.

If I couldn't get out of the rope, I'd die.

They didn't want my death on their heads, did they?

Which meant they might come back and make sure I wasn't still hanging under the tree.

It was a thought that scared me the whole time I was there this morning.

They might've shown up at any second.

I climbed the boulder, anyway, brought down my water bottle and ran. Didn't even waste time looking for my knife.

A great, safe feeling to be back here at my secret camp.

Except for my journal, everything's packed and ready to go.

Only one problem. I don't know *where* to go.

I should start heading back for the car. I only brought ten days of food, and this is day six. (Haven't been eating as much as planned, though. I could stretch things out.) Another reason to start for the car is that Gloria and Susie went the *other* way. Turning back, I won't run afoul of them again.

Which is also a good reason *not* to turn back.

It's crazy. But the thing is, I can't get Gloria out of my head.

I've got to find her.

Now that I think about it, maybe she'll come to me.

And maybe she won't. I just spent a few hours "hanging."

Figuring the gals might return to make sure I wasn't still tied, I went back to where they'd camped. Hid my stuff. Put on my jacket, stepped under the branch, reached behind myself and took hold of the rope.

It seemed like a good idea.

Made me awfully hot and tired, but I stuck with it. Then some hikers appeared. I spotted them when they came around a bend in the trail. Fortunately, they were still a long distance off. I had plenty of time to gather my stuff and hide.

They left the trail and headed for the lake.

I stayed just long enough to see that all three were guys.

So much for "hanging around" and waiting for the girls.

Thought I might spend the night at Little Boy Lake, after all. So I stopped by its shore, ate some supper, and now I'm bringing things up to date.

This lake really sucks. It's so desolate it gives me the heebie-jeebies. No way will I spend a night here.

Guess I'll just start walking, even though it'll be dark soon. See how far I can get before petering out—or falling off the trail and breaking my head open, ha ha.

June 23

Spent most of last night hiking. The trail led along desolate granite slopes. The bright moon painted the rocks white. All around, boulders draped patches of the ground with black shadows. The shadows didn't frighten me, though. I saw them as friendly places where I might duck and hide if someone should invade my solitude.

The only sound was the wind except when a stream was nearby. The rushy noise made by the wind was hard to tell from the noise of fast moving water.

I met nobody at all on the trail.

Did see some coyotes. Being gray, they were

just barely visible in the moonlight. Ghostly. They didn't scare me, though. We shared the night and the wilds. I thought how neat it would be to run with them.

They wanted no part of that. When I put down my pack, they vanished. I went ahead and stripped down, anyway, and ran alone. The wind felt wonderful. I climbed rocks to a high summit. Standing at the top, I was washed in moonlight, rubbed by the wind.

In my head, I pictured Gloria atop the summit. Gloria standing there instead of me, naked, skin like cream in the moonlight, hair streaming behind her. I pictured myself moving in behind her, fitting my body against hers, feeling her hair in my face, filling my hands with her breasts.

At dawn, I spread out my sleeping bag beside a stream and slept. Awoke when the sun was high, built a fire, made coffee and a stew. After eating, I spent a while enjoying the icy water of the stream. Later, I sprawled out in the sunlight to dry. I slept some more, then dug out my journal.

Now I'm caught up again.

Don't know what to do next.

Keep going, I guess. Even if I can't find Gloria again, I would rather go deeper into the wilds than return to my car.

Where are Gloria and Susie? It seems like I should've overtaken them by now. They *can't* still be ahead of me. I've gone too far, too fast, for that. They must've headed off on a side trail, unless I passed them without knowing.

Nobody seems to be around this area except me.

I've found a good, hidden place among the rocks above the trail. From here, I can see anyone who might come along.

I'm eager for darkness to arrive—ready for a romp.

June 24

Last night was great. Ran in the moonlight. Climbed. But also spent a lot of time motionless, listening and watching. If you stand still for a very long time, you feel yourself being absorbed by the wilderness.

You start to feel that you are becoming part of it all.

June 28

Hell, journal. Long time, no see.

I've gone quite a distance since my last entry. Not on the trail, though. Just around.

Romping.

So much better out here without lugging a backpack. Left it hidden, then came and went. Came back only for food, and to flake out.

Haven't seen Gloria or Susie. God knows where they've gone, but I probably won't see them again. That's all right. Gloria was glorious. Best that she's gone, though.

Who needs her, anyway?

Who needs anyone, when you have the whole wilderness to yourself and when you have complete freedom?

Nothing could be better than this.

The only problem is my shortage of food. This is day twelve. Still have some left, but it won't last long. I'm about an eight-day hike from the car, ha ha.

Who cares?

I would very much enjoy sinking my teeth into a bacon cheeseburger. The only other thing I crave is a chocolate milkshake.

Not sure what I'll do when the food runs out.

June 29

Packed up this morning and hit the trail. Very strange to be dressed and carrying a backpack again. Like I've left some of my freedom behind. But also like I'm an imposter.

Might've stayed where I was, except for the food situation.

Over time, maybe I can learn to live off the land. Or maybe not. I don't know what might

be edible up here in the roots and berries department. Obviously, animals and fish could be eaten.
I'd have to catch them first, though. I don't even
have a knife anymore.

Last night, a solution came to me.

I need to find other campers and get food from
them.

So now I'm on my way to Blackwood Lake. It
looks pretty big on the map. With any luck, I'll
find some people there.

My lucky day, all right. Reached Blackwood Lake
a few minutes ago. Saw three tents together
among the trees near the shore, and several people
standing near a fire. I could smell the woodsmoke.
And I could smell something with a wonderful
onion aroma. Perhaps a soup they were preparing.

Going over now for a little recon.

I crept as close to the camp as I dared, and watched
from behind a tree. A quick look was enough to
tell me these weren't people I wanted to steal from.
The gathering looked like a reunion of the Mean
and Ugly Clan.

There were three adult males who *had* to be
brothers. One was skinny, one a tub of lard and
one buffed up like a bodybuilder, but they all had
the same droopy eyes, sneery mouths and jug ears.
They all had black hair, too. Some of the pony
tails were longer than others. None of the three

wore a shirt. Skinny and Fatso both had tattoos all over their arms, backs and chests. Not Muscles, though. His skin was uncarved, unscarred. Unlike the other two, he was also without earrings. Each guy wore blue jeans, a wide leather belt, and a big hunting knife in a sheath.

The women were prizes, too.

One had a butt as wide as a refrigerator. It was packed into jeans, while her upper acres wore only a denim vest. Her arms were tattooed from shoulder to wrist. When she turned in my direction, I saw that her vest was wide open, spread apart by enormous melon breasts. At first, I thought she might be wearing a skin-tight, brightly patterned shirt under the vest. She wasn't, though. Beneath her vest was nothing but a garment of tattoos.

The other gal had a slim body and a long, horsey face with big slabs of front teeth jutting out from under her upper lip. Her hair was cut so short it looked like a two-day growth of whiskers. She wore big hoop earrings. She also wore a grimy white T-shirt that hung just a little lower than her crotch. No pants, no underwear, no shoes, no nothing except that flimsy old shirt. I could pretty much see through it. She was borderline ugly. She looked dirty and dumb and sour. But I couldn't help getting all turned on by her.

She and the others were hanging around the campfire. On its grill was a big pot with steam drifting up. This was probably full of soup or stew. It had a strong onion smell. Nobody talked. Muscles sometimes drew his knife and gave the concoction a stir. The others occasionally took turns adding wood to the fire. The gal in the T-shirt did it a few times, crouching and leaning forward while she tossed twigs onto the flames. I didn't get to see anything except her butt, though.

Finally, I decided to get while the getting was good.

Keeping low, I backed away from the tree. Then turned around and crept off. By the time I dared to glance behind me, a thick array of bushes and trees hid the bunch from my sight. Figured I'd made a clean getaway.

Very relieved, I hurried around a high clump of rock.

And stopped dead.

She had big blue eyes. They got even bigger and her mouth dropped open.

She was ready to yell.

I had a quick memory of being at the mercy of Gloria and Susie—how they'd had me helpless, could've done *anything* to me.

If *this* bunch decided to punish me . . .

I stopped the gal from yelling.

Threw myself at her, jammed the palm of my hand against her open mouth, caught her throat with my other hand and slammed her down backward, me on top. The ground knocked her wind out. She grunted into my palm. Before she could put up any fight, I let go of her mouth. Gripped her neck with both hands, raised her head toward me, and shot it down. I knew we were on granite, not soft dirt. That didn't stop me, though. Her head smacked the granite. *Whock!* I gave it one more bounce, just for insurance, even though the first had taken her out of the picture.

After that, I spent a while lying on her and gazing over my shoulder, ready to scurry up and run for my life. But nobody seemed to be coming. No voices cried out. All I heard were birds and the rushy noise of the wind.

The same thing kept going through my head. *I've done it now. I've done it now. Oh boy oh boy, I've done it now.*

The gal was unconscious. Not dead, though. I could feel her breathing.

I didn't know what to do.

Run?

But she would wake up and tell on me, and they would hunt for me. All my nifty pretenses about being invisible suddenly seemed like nonsense. If that bunch came after me, they would find me. They'd be eager to get revenge for my attack on this one. They'd do horrible, unspeakable things to me—I was sure of that.

On the other hand, they wouldn't hunt for me, wouldn't even be aware of my existence, if this one simply vanished.

They'd think she had wandered off, maybe gotten herself lost, or even split for reasons of her own.

If they searched, they would search for her—not for me.

The solution to my problem was obvious.

Take her with me.

I had to do it. No choice in the matter. But I *wanted* to do it, too.

Take her with me.

Yes!

First, I crawled off her. She was sprawled on the ground, arms out, legs apart, head turned as if to look past her shoulder, though her eyes were shut. She had long hair the color of hay. It stuck out all over the place as if it hadn't been touched by a comb or brush in about five years. Her face wouldn't win any prizes, but it didn't look too bad. A small, white scar curved upward from one corner of her mouth. It gave her a smirk. There was something about it that made me feel a little sad for her.

She didn't look any older than me, whereas the rest of her bunch seemed to be closing in on thirty. She might've been a daughter. More likely, she was a runaway or something who had fallen in with one of them.

She was barefoot, like the T-shirt gal. Her legs were slim and dark. They looked healthy, somehow, in spite of their numerous nicks and scabs and bruises. Her cut-off blue jeans were faded almost white, ragged, with threads hanging like fringe against her thighs. The cut-offs basically had no legs at all. The crotch was gone except for a narrow strip of denim that drooped between her thighs. She wore the jeans very low. Her leather belt was higher, buckled around bare skin, slanting downward from above her left hip. Her knife was sheathed below her right hip. The damn thing looked like a Bowie knife.

I pulled it out.

After all, she might wake up while I was carrying her.

I wasn't sure where to put it, though. Someplace out of her reach.

The top she wore was a dirty gray sweatshirt. Its sleeves had gone the way of her jeans legs, leaving her shoulders bare and leaving big, droopy holes under her armpits. Her shoulders and arms looked pretty banged up—bruised and scraped as if maybe she had taken a tumble off some rocks. The bottom half of the sweatshirt had been lopped off just below her breasts. I could see their smooth round undersides.

Though mighty tempted to snag the sweatshirt up a little higher, I held off. This was no place to let myself get carried away. Not with her clan so nearby.

Clamping the knife between my teeth (not easy, it being a big, heavy monster), I took hold of the gal's shoulders and pulled her toward me, lifting her to a sitting position. From there, I wrestled her to her feet. Bracing her up, I took the knife out of my teeth. Then I ducked and she slumped over my shoulder.

Off we went.

I jogged for a while. Kept the knife in my right hand, and had my left arm hooked across the backs of her legs, hugging her thighs to my chest. With every stride, she bounced on my shoulder. She flopped against my back a lot, too.

I kept checking behind us. From the looks of things, we were in the clear.

I walked on the trail for a while, going slowly and trying to recover. From the loose feel of the gal, she still seemed to be unconscious. She swayed from side to side with the motion of my strides. My T-shirt was very thin and sweaty and clinging to me, so I could tell that her sweatshirt must've fallen away from her breasts. They rubbed across my back. I could feel their heat and how they were soft and firm and springy. After a while, I lifted my shirt so I could have them against my bare skin. It was great. They were smooth and slick. I could even feel the nipples sliding against my back like small tongues.

I couldn't wait to get her off the trail and hidden somewhere good and secluded.

Finally, a broad, shallow stream crossed the trail. I carried my prisoner upstream. Climbed higher and higher. Sometimes, when the way became too steep, I detoured off to one side or another and forged easier routes.

At last, I found a place close to the stream where the mountainside is somewhat level. Natural rock formations wall off the front and sides. It is the best hiding place I have found so far. It is perfect.

That's where I am writing this.

I left her alone for a while and hurried all the way back to Blackwood Lake. It was closer than I thought. Distances seem ten times as great when you're carrying someone. Still, I figure that our stream crosses the trail no less than a mile from where I grabbed her. I think we're safe.

At Blackwood Lake, I stayed well clear of the weirdos. Saw some smoke from their fire, but that was all. Grabbed my pack and got the hell away from there.

I was totally pooped by the time I got back here.

The gal looked as if she hadn't moved at all.

Dusk, now. Almost dark.

I've been writing forever—a couple of hours, anyway. Catching up while I keep an eye on her.

She's still unconscious.

I hope she'll be all right.

It would solve certain problems if she died. I don't want to even think about that, though.

She seems prettier now. Kind of sweet and vulnerable, like a sleeping kid.

I crawled over to her. I hadn't bothered to fix her sweatshirt after putting her down, so it had been rumpled up above her breasts the whole time.

I gave her a pretty good looking over. This was the first time I'd ever been so close to a woman who was the next best thing to naked. I studied her close up and checked out all the details. I won't go into it here. Could write pages and pages, but my hand is already tired of all this scribbling. One thing, though—from what I saw of her tan, she'd spent a lot of time outside with nothing on. She had a fabulous body, and I tried to imagine how great she must look if she weren't so banged up.

At one point, I used my knife on that little strip of denim between her legs. I cut it off so that nothing would be in the way. That's pretty much what finished it.

I saw her there unconscious and me crouching over her, knife in hand, *messing* with her. It turned my insides cold.

So I quit it all. I pulled her sweatshirt down over her breasts. I took my T-shirt and spread it like a big napkin to hide her crotch.

Then I crawled over to my pack, dug out the spiral notebook and started to write.

God, is my hand sore.

Can hardly see what I'm writing, now, because of the darkness. All caught up, anyway.

June 30

It's morning. The girl is still unconscious. She's not dead, though. It's as if she's asleep. I tried to wake her up, but she wouldn't come out of it.

I ate the last of my food last night—except for one chocolate bar, which I will save for the girl.

It got cold last night after the sun went down. I wrestled the girl into my sleeping bag so that she wouldn't freeze. Put on my jacket, climbed to where I had a view down the mountainside, and kept watch.

Later, I turned in. Tight quarters in my sleeping bag. I was pretty tempted and excited, but didn't want to end up feeling dirty so I rolled and put my back to the girl without so much as copping a feel.

I could feel how she pressed against my backside, but that was unavoidable so I was free to like it and not have any guilt.

Got an awful shock. I wrote that last stuff in camp, then wandered over to the stream. Stripped and jumped in, splashed around for a while till the water threatened to freeze me blue. Then I climbed out and sprawled in the sunlight.

I was never more than twenty or thirty feet from my sleeping bag, where I'd left the gal. But when I stood up and turned around, the bag was open and empty.

No sign of her.

Gone! A trapdoor snapped open low inside me, and my stomach dropped.

In a frenzy, I ran this way and that, searching for her as my mind tried to deal with the situation. I climbed rocks. I leaped crannies. I hunted high and low.

Not a trace of her.

Of course not. She hadn't ducked into a hiding place, she'd run for her life. Down the slope, no doubt, and back down the trail toward Blackwood Lake.

Back to her cronies.

If she'd snuck off the moment I headed for the stream, she could've reached them by the time I even realized she was missing. They could already be on their way to my camp.

I scurried up the rocks to my lookout. The trail below was clear.

But they might not *come* by the trail.

My first thought was to hide. Hide fast.

But suppose there might still be time to head off the girl? After all, she'd suffered a major head injury. Didn't seem likely that she would wake up full of energy. Hell, no. She'd probably be weak and dizzy. Even disoriented. Maybe even with a good case of amnesia.

Plenty of reasons for hope.

I didn't take time to dress. Got into my trunks, pushed my bare feet into my sneakers, snatched up her huge knife and raced to find her. Followed the stream down, figuring it was her most likely route to the trail. No sign of her, though.

No sign of her on the trail, either. No sign of anyone.

As I neared Blackwood Lake, the idea came that maybe her friends had already broken camp and gone away. Would they do that, though? Just leave without her? I sure hadn't noticed them searching for her. If they *had* searched, they'd never ventured anywhere close to our stream.

Maybe they were glad to be rid of her.

Anyway, I really hoped they had moved on.

But they hadn't.

I stayed on the trail until the tents came into view. Crept into the trees for a better look. Their campsite appeared deserted, but plenty of gear was scattered around. The fire was smoldering. From the looks of the place, the bunch had just gone away for a while.

Gone on a little "search and destroy" mission, perhaps.

Weird, but I didn't feel very scared just then. I felt relieved that they were gone. And somewhat amazed that we hadn't run into each other. (Had they taken a back route above the trail?) Also, I felt disappointed and betrayed by the girl, which is ridiculous. How could she have known that I'd kept my hands off her, that I'd actually *cared* about her?

Anyway, they had left their camp unattended and I was out of food.

After watching and listening for a while just to avoid any surprises, I made my way into the heart of their camp. Backpacks were propped upright here and there, two of them against stumps near the fireplace. I went for those two and chose the blue one on the left.

Still had the girl's knife, so I slid it under the elastic waistband of my trunks. Off to the side, by my hip. The elastic was hardly strong enough to hold it up. My trunks kind of sagged on that side, and I could feel the weight of the warm blade against my skin.

Once the knife was out of my way, I started digging into the backpack. Found a treasure of freeze-dried food.

There was no reason to act cagey about the theft. They knew all about me, thanks to the girl. So I upended the pack. Dumped everything, then began to refill it with just food.

I'd tossed in an almost weightless can of dried beef, a heavy pouch of powdered eggs, and a bag of nuts when Max showed up.

At the time, I didn't know her name.

I didn't know who or what was coming, just heard huffing sounds and feet crunching across the rug of old leaves and pine needles on their way toward my back.

Going sick with fright, I spun around.

RICHARD LAYMON

It was the fat, tattooed woman with the hair helmet. She carried a roll of toilet paper, which told me where she'd been. Off somewhere answering nature's call, not hunting for me.

She didn't ask who I was, or what I thought I was doing in her camp. She didn't yell for help. She didn't scream. She just grinned and kept coming.

Grinned, flung her toilet paper aside, and shucked off her denim vest.

Above her belt, she was a flopping mass of tattooed flesh. I glimpsed vines, vultures, daggers and skulls. Bright coral snakes coiled around each of her huge, bouncing breasts.

At first, I couldn't do anything but stare at her. Amazed. Terrified. Then I took off. Ran like hell for the lake, with Max pounding after me.

Real quick, I found out why people carry their knives inside sheaths. I was okay for a few strides, but then the blade started slicing into the side of my leg. It cut me again and again and again as I dashed for the lake. Then I couldn't stand it anymore and snatched out the knife.

Wasn't too careful about it, either. In my rush to jerk the knife out of harm's way, I slashed my trunks.

About that time, water started splashing up my legs. I had a pretty good lead on Max. I figured to run out a bit father, then dive and swim away from her. But the plan went to hell when I pulled the knife. The trunks went loose, slipped down and grabbed me around the thighs. I fell sprawling. Smacked the water. Before I could push myself up, she was on me.

She dragged my trunks all the way down and off. She flipped me over onto my back. She dropped to her knees between my legs and grabbed my butt with both hands and hauled me up out of the water. She didn't even glance at my face, just kept her eyes on my dick, panting as she pulled me higher. Then she licked her lips and bowed down.

Maybe she wanted to suck me off.

Maybe she wanted to bite me off.

I never found out which. I put my knife into her left eye.

As I already wrote, it was a very big knife.

It stopped a few inches in when the blade got too wide for her eye socket. It got kind of caught in the bone hole, and I had a hard time pulling it out. Her head jerked every which way while I worked on removing the knife. The whole time, stuff kept pouring out of the socket onto my belly and groin. Not just blood, but glop and pieces of bone.

At last, I got the knife out of her. I shoved her away, then scurried out to deeper water and washed myself off.

I was pretty grossed out, actually.

And petrified. Now I'd *killed* one of these throw-backs. There'd be hell to pay.

I had to get out of there.

Get while the gettin's good.

What the hell is that, *Get while the gettin's good?* Anyway, it went through my head like a chant— get while the gettin's good, get while the gettin's good—over and over again as I scanned the shore in a panic and splashed my way out of the water and ran into their camp.

Told myself to calm down. The others wouldn't be back for a while. When they couldn't find me at the place by the stream, they'd probably search around for a while. I had time.

So I threw some more food into the backpack. Held the knife between my teeth to leave my hands free. Which made breathing hard. After a while, it made my jaw ache. A very big, heavy knife.

When I had enough food to last me a couple of weeks, I swung the pack onto my back.

Gotta get while the gettin's good.

Right.

I took the knife out of my mouth and stood there, taking deep breaths.

Gotta get!

There was a single, logical place to go. Back to my car. A long journey, but from there I could drive away and be safe. No other course of action *would* be safe. My only chance for survival, it seemed, was to drive out of the wilds, back to civilization.

And I'd better get started fast.

Get while the gettin's good.

God only knows why I stayed put. I just stood there with the pack on my back and the knife in my hand, staring at nothing in particular while I tried to make up my mind.

Maybe I *had* made up my mind, but just hadn't admitted it yet.

It felt a little as if I was in a trance.

I got to feeling very calm, and didn't even get worked up when the voices came.

At the sound of the voices, I unshouldered the pack and eased it to the ground. I ducked inside one of the tents. It was a red tent. The sun came through, filling the air with ruddy light. It made my skin look red. Two sleeping bags were spread out side by side. I turned myself around so I faced the front, lay down flat in the middle and put one eye to the narrow gap between the flaps.

I had a while to wait. The sleeping bags felt soft and nice under me, but the air was heavy, stifling. The tent was like a car parked in the sunlight, its windows shut. Sweat poured off me. It tickled. It stung my eyes. It made the handle of the knife slippery.

Beyond the gap, dust motes swirled in the

sunlight. A chipmunk atop a shadowed rock reared up and gazed toward the lake. I saw the leaves of a bush near the fireplace shiver with the touch of a breeze.

The stifling air smelled of pine and old dry wood, mixed with a faint but pungent odor of plastic from the tent and sleeping bags. There was also a sweetish aroma of insect repellent.

I watched an ant crawl across a twig a few inches beyond the tent opening.

I heard everything.

I heard myself. Each breath trembled. My heart thumped very loud. I heard the blood surging through every vessel in my body. My eyelids made soft, wet clicking sounds when I blinked. Each dribble of sweat whispered a soft hiss as it skidded down my skin.

Those were my sounds, but not the only sounds. Off in the distance, gulls squealed. The wind made a long *shhhhhh*. Near and far, bugs hummed and buzzed. The voices got louder.

There would be Skinny, Fatso, and Muscles. There would be T-shirt girl and My Girl.

My Girl?

I wished.

Me against five.

It was very likely that I would be killed.

I thought about that Indian who was about to go into battle (maybe at the Little Big Horn?) and supposedly said, "It is a good day to die." But I think maybe he was full of shit—that there's no such thing as a good day to die.

I decided that there are good *places* to die, though.

This was a good, peaceful place. The idea of being dead here didn't seem terrible. Not in the tent, but out in the open. I would be a body on the ground like the bodies of dead insects, dead birds, trees that had fallen and were gradually becoming part of the ground. All of us slowly becoming part of things. Blending in.

It seemed all right. It seemed almost perfect.

But then they walked into camp, talking calmly. And terror squeezed me.

Their voices suddenly changed.

"Holy shit!" one blurted.

The other yelled, "Max!"

They ran past the tent.

Two of them. Skinny and Fatso. As they ran by, Skinny threw down the easel he'd been carrying. He propped a canvas against a rock with a certain amount of care, while Fatso simply dropped his wooden box. The box was the size of a small suitcase, and I found later that it was loaded with tubes of paint, a palette, brushes, rags and other odds and ends an artist might need for depicting mountain scenery.

In a moment, the two guys were out of sight.

I crawled from the tent. Nobody else was there. The air felt fool, delicious.

They stood at the edge of the lake, apparently staring at Max. She was a few yards out on the water, floating on her back.

They wore jeans, but no shirts. Their backs and arms were acrawl with green and blue and red tattoos.

Skinny heard me first. When he started to turn around, I chopped the side of his neck with my Bowie knife. The blade made a soft thump. I had no trouble pulling it out. It left a deep raw wedge that sprayed blood.

He yelled and grabbed the wound and kept turning around. I elbowed him out of my way. As he stumbled backward, I went for the Fatso. He squealed like a woman and put out his hands and backed away from me. He was almost as floppy as Max.

I went after him. He said things like, "What's the *matter* with you?" and "Why are you doing this?" and "Leave me alone!" and "Don't hurt me! Please, please, don't hurt me."

He kept his hands out in front of him to ward off the knife.

They got awfully hacked up. He lost a few fingers. He had the head of a screaming woman tattooed on his big old belly. She looked like Medusa. When I finally got past his hands, I put the blade right into Medusa's mouth.

His own mouth made a tight little O and he said, "Oooooo."

I pulled the knife out and he dropped onto his butt.

Then Skinny came at me from behind. He was bloody all over, and wet from falling into the lake. He wasn't in very good shape anymore. I put the knife in under his chin so hard it lifted him to his tiptoes.

After that, I finished off both of them.

Three down, three to go.

I felt great. Better maybe than I'd ever felt before. And more excited, too.

I should've been scared about going after the rest of them—especially Muscles. The guy was big and buffed and could probably take me apart with his bare hands. I should've been terrified. But I *looked forward* to nailing him. I relished the idea.

Not as much, though, as I relished the idea of getting the two gals.

I couldn't wait.

So after washing the blood off me, I went looking for them. I scurried and crept, stealthy as a savage. And found the others in a cove near the south end of the lake.

Not *all* the others. Just Muscles and the T-shirt girl. The girl I wanted most—my former captive—was still missing.

The two I found were together on a slab of granite that slanted down into the water.

Today, the gal wore a bright orange T-shirt. She sat with her back straight, her legs crossed, a fishing pole in her hands. Her line was in the water. She used one of those bobbers that's like a small plastic ball. It drifted on the water a few feet in front of the rock ledge where she sat.

She wasn't watching her bobber. Her head was turned toward Muscles, just over to her right.

He was doing push-ups.

He wore leopard skin bikini pants. With every push-up, muscles bulged and writhed under his gleaming tanned hide.

I trembled as I watched him.

He was a sleek and powerful beast. My prey.

He did forty push-ups just while I was watching, and he was still at it when I hurried away.

I came back a little while later in the water, steering Max beside me. She floated very well on her back. I guided her with the knife, which I'd plunged in under her shoulder blade. He body made a good holder for the knife, and the knife made a good handle for propelling her alongside me.

I kept her body between myself and the shore.

I had my head just beneath her armpit and close to her body. There, I not only had the thickness of her upper torso for shelter, but also the great hills of her beautifully decorated breasts.

My head was basically wedged into the soft V

between her thick upper arm and her side. Her skin felt slippery and very cold against my face.

Concealed by my barge of tattooed female flesh and fat, I made my way toward the cove.

We stayed far out.

I could see nothing except Max. She had no tattoos on her side. That stretch was a clean slate of shiny skin as white as a fish belly.

"How's the water out there, Maxine?" called a voice I took for that of the T-shirt gal.

Maxine, of course, ignored her.

"Yo! Y'deaf?" A few moments passed. Then, in a voice that wasn't so loud, she said, "Hey, Miles. Miles! Cut it out. There's something the matter with Max." Another pause. "See? She doesn't wanta move or nothing. And look at her eye. There's something funny about her eye."

The funny thing about Max's eye was that it was Fatso's eye. It had been a major improvement over her raw empty socket. I hadn't given the whole thing much thought—putting in a fresh eye had seemed like a good idea. Guess I wanted my decoy to look alive.

I won't go into all the gory details. I did a fast and messy job, got Fatso's eye out in one piece (his face wouldn't win any prizes afterward, ha ha), but I kind of screwed the eye up when I tried to shove it into Max's socket. Anyway, I got it in, but the thing ended up looking a bit shriveled and crooked.

Miles said, "Yeah. Looks kinda fucked up." Then he called, "Max! Are you okay? What's wrong with you?"

Pretty soon, the gal said, "She isn't dead, is she?"

"Naaah."

"She kind of looks dead."

"Naaah, she's fine."

"She doesn't look *very* fine."

Miles shouted, "Damn it, Max!" He sounded steamed.

"You'd better go in and get her."

"*You* go in and get her if you want her so bad."

"I can't swim, and you know it. If I could swim, I would. I think she's dead. We can't just leave her in there. What if she sinks?"

"She's too fat to sink," Miles said.

"Maybe she pitched a heart attack."

"That'd surprise the hell out of me. Her cardio-vascular system's gotta be shot to shit. I'm surprised she didn't drop dead years ago, the cow."

"Shhhh. What if she hears you?"

"I thought you said she's dead."

"I don't *know* she's dead. She just isn't moving, that's all. And her eye. Does a heart attack fuck up your eye?"

"Maybe we better go find Doug and Louie."

"Don't be such a wimp. Go in and get her."

"Let Louie do it. She's *his* wife. Sides, he swims better than me."

"That's a hell of a note. What good are all those muscles of yours if you can't even . . ."

"They're *dense*, hon. They weigh me down like rocks."

"If you *had* any rocks, you'd quit whining and go after her."

"Okay, okay. Jeez! Chill. I'll do it. Okay?"

I waited to hear a splash.

Instead of a splash, I heard Miles say, "It's freezing, Liz!"

"You big baby!"

"Okay, okay!"

At last, the splash. From the sounds of churning water, Miles was swimming toward me on the surface.

I tugged my knife out of Max, then took a deep breath and ducked underneath her. My eyes were open, so I could see up through the water. The sunlight came in at an angle, bands of it slanting down like the blades of golden swords. Except you could see through these blades, and they were full of swirling specks—dust and bugs and bits of dead stuff. It was lovely to look at, but sort of made you want to take a bath.

Then Miles came along.

He was swimming, stretched out straight, blocking the sunlight, churning the water with a pretty good form when I got him.

Put my knife into his belly button and shoved

up. The knife punched into him, but the shove thrust me downward, too. I went down so fast that the blade pulled right out of him.

It got a little crazy after that. (Maybe it had gotten a little crazy *before* that, ha ha.)

Anyway, Miles grabbed onto Max and tried to climb on her as if she were a life raft and if he could only board her, he'd be all right. But she couldn't hold his weight up. She sank and rolled. The two of them looked like wrestlers.

He should've been wrestling with me, not her.

Lucky break for me.

I caught hold of his ponytail. Hanging onto that so I wouldn't go scooting away again, I stabbed him a few times in the back. Then I cut his throat.

I surfaced on the other side of Max. That way, I could grab some air without Liz seeing me. She sounded hysterical. She was yelling stuff like "Miles! What's going on! Stop it! If you think you're being funny, you're not! Miles!"

Then I swam under Max and over Miles. He was sinking, so maybe he'd been right about his muscles being as heavy as rocks. He was going lower and lower, ribbons of blood curling up from his throat. A tiny fish, flashing silver in the faint light, darted in at his neck and nibbled a shred of something.

Miles looked as if he planned to sit on the bottom. He was all wavery and shimmery. His head was back. He seemed to be watching me. Both his arms were raised toward me, and the fingertips of one hand stroked my thigh as I swam over him.

His touch sent goose bumps racing all over my skin.

I liked it.

I swam underwater all the way, then reached high and grabbed the edge of granite and burst through the surface—up into the hot air and sunlight in an explosion of spray.

Liz was squatting about six feet away. She glanced at me, then lowered her head. She reached down between her knees and rummaged through a rusty green tackle box.

I scurried onto the granite slab and went for her.

Letting out a cross between a whine and a growl, she sprang up and hurled the tackle box at me. The instant it left her hands, she spun around and ran.

My left arm whacked the tackle box away. But out jumped everything; a stringer, needle-nosed pliers, the Swiss Army knife that Liz had probably been searching for, plus leaders and weights and bobbers and hooks, small jars of bait, rubber worms, and a collection of artificial lures.

Most of the stuff either missed me or bounced off.

Nothing really hurt me.

Except the lures.

Beautiful, sparkling bright decoys shaped like small fish, most about the size of my thumb. Some were outfitted with silvery spoons to make them jig in the water. Others had spinners, and some had squidlike rubber tentacles. From every last one of the lures dangled no less than three small grappling hooks.

I don't know how many lures hit me. But six of them stuck.

They hit, then started to fall, then found pieces of my bare skin to snag with their barbed hooks.

One pierced my shoulder, one my upper arm. Another hooked my left nipple. Another got me at the knob of my hip bone. One caught my thigh. And then there was the big silver minnow that dropped onto my boner. It lay there like a guy trying to shinny up a tree trunk. Its barbs gripped me like tiny, sharp fingernails. I clamped the knife between my teeth, then used both hands and very carefully removed it.

Couldn't even *think* about Liz until that was taken care of.

She should've used the opportunity to run. Instead, she only backed away as if she were afraid to take her eyes off me.

I threw away the damn minnow, decided I could live with the rest of the lures, snatched the knife out of my teeth and went for her.

That's when she turned tail and ran.

But it was too late.

I raced after her, leaping from rock to rock, then chasing her through the trees. She headed in the direction of her campsite. Maybe she thought Louie and Doug would save her.

The lures were a nuisance. They dangled and bounced like weird ornaments, digging their hooks in deeper, grabbing on with more barbs. I bled. My wounds hurt. But none of that slowed me down.

Liz was halfway across a sunny clearing when I got her. A shove between her shoulder blades threw her headlong out of control. She hit the ground and skidded. Then she rolled onto her back and kicked and flapped her arms at me, trying to keep me away.

She didn't have anything on except for the pink T-shirt. Its front bounced and jumped and swung all over the place, thrown by her breasts. She was naked below the waist.

I kicked her in the head. Then I sat on her and cut the T-shirt open down the front.

Cora and I broke up before we ever got a chance to make love. I'd wanted her awfully badly. And I'd wanted Gloria. And the blonde girl whose name I didn't even know, but who had spent the night unconscious with me in my sleeping bag. I'd ached for each of them. But I'd never *had* any of them.

I'd never *had* any girl at all.

So here now finally was my big chance.

Liz was dazed, helpless. She had hurt me with the lures. And she had to die, anyway.

It was perfect.

I stayed sitting on her while I worked the hooks out of my skin and set aside the lures. Then I got between her legs. Kneeling there, I fooled around with her—caressing her, squeezing her, pinching her, delving into her with my fingers. But when I was about to shove my cock into her, all of a sudden I went sick inside.

I might be a lot of things, but I'm not a rapist.

To fuck a stranger like this while she was almost unconscious and completely helpless went against everything. It would've been crossing the line.

So I didn't do it.

My principles wouldn't allow it.

All I did was give her some payback with the fishing lures. That got her wide awake fast. Then I started using the knife on her. She screamed a lot. By the time she died, I was worn out. I sprawled on the ground next to her, and slept.

Later, I returned to the lake and washed off the blood and stuff.

I took what I wanted from the camp. Including a whole backpack full of food and an artist's sketch pad that I will be able to use when my spiral notebook runs out of paper. I took a lot of things, actually.

Making all the bodies and equipment disappear would've been too much trouble, so I didn't even try.

I didn't even look for that last girl, either.

It dawned on me that the group at Blackwood Lake had only five packs and five sleeping bags. The girl I'd taken prisoner probably hadn't been one of them, after all. No idea who she is, or what she was doing near their camp when we ran into each other.

She seems to be gone, though.

Alas.

Anyway, I returned with my booty to my camp by the stream. In spite of all that had happened, it was still quite early in the day when I got here.

I spent the remainder of the afternoon catching up on the journal. Man, I sure did have a lot of catching up to do!

I'd write for an hour, then go for a dip in the swift, cold stream, then sprawl in the sun, then write some more. Once in a while, I climbed my lookout rock for a quick check around.

This is a very desolate area. Except for the bunch by Blackwood Lake—and the girl—I've seen nobody since arriving here. Hope it stays that way. It would be very handy if the bodies don't get discovered until I'm gone.

Tomorrow, I'll head north.

Plenty of food, thanks to the clan by the lake.

Maybe I'll just hike on through the wilds forever.

July 1

Shit shit shit shit!

I was all set to hit the trail this morning, but someone's *stolen my fucking journal!!!*

I've still got this artist's pad, so I'm not entirely out of luck, but—

I think I want to throw up.

The journal told *everything*! All about the killings—they were self-defense, really. Those creeps would've killed me if I'd let them.

I think the fucking journal *has my name in it*!

Holy fucking shit!

Not on the cover, but inside. There was something about me being like the Deerslayer or Pathfinder or something—what a joke.

Guess I can claim the journal is fiction.

Shit!

All I can imagine is that the girl took it. No other explanation. I'd left it inside my pack, so it didn't just *blow* away. A chipmunk didn't fucking eat it for lunch. Shit!

What'll she do with it?

If she gives it to the cops, I'm cooked.

I don't know whether I'm in California or Nevada. California has the death penalty. I don't know whether there's capital punishment in Nevada. Maybe Nevada is too civilized for that kind of shit.

I'm in such deep shit.

I've got to find that girl and get my journal back. I've got to!

Dear Ned Champion,

Thanks for the loan of your journal. Sorry to put you through such a panic, but I saw you writing in it all day after you came back from the lake, and I felt compelled to peruse it. I enjoyed it thoroughly (in spite of my headache, thank you very much) and I'm sure you're pleased to have it back. You sure did look high and low for it—though in all the wrong places.

You've met your match, fellow.

I'm the wildest, cagiest, and easily the most invisible girl in the Sierras.

My name is Lynn.

You came to the correct conclusion about me: i.e., I was not a member of the Blackwood Lake party. Not even close. It certainly took you long enough to arrive at that conclusion, however.

Actually, I feel a trifle hurt that you ever mistook me for one of them. Circumstantial evidence apparently prevailed. And, after all, we never did have a chance to converse. So you went by my location—and by my appearance?

Thanks a heap for your kind words about my face, by the way. A girl sure does enjoy reading that she isn't "any prize." Obviously, however, you were rather impressed by the bod. (I like your's, too. Yes, indeed!)

Sincere thanks for showing such restraint in the area of "messing" with me. I mean that. I am very grateful. From what you wrote (and the evidence of my cut-offs), the temptation was great. Congratulations for resisting. You're a bit strange, but you have a streak of appealing gallantry.

Interesting that you didn't "have" Liz, either. I've seen her body. She might've preferred your penis.

You sure did make a mess of those people, by the way.

Again, congratulations.

I ran afoul of that bunch almost a week ago. I was camping alone at Blackwood Lake when they showed up.

Right, alone.

You're not the only one, you know.

I came out to the mountains after finals. I was a sophomore at Stanford. Of course, that was last summer.

I never went back. From what I read in your journal, it appears that you went through much the same transformation that I did—except for the difference that my changes began a year ago. I'm still out here, still enjoying the wild life. And getting wilder all the time (ha ha, as you like to write—which I find to be a rather annoying affectation. We'll have to work on your style.)

But I digress.

I have been out here for more than a year now. I have a cave for the winter. It's well stocked with all sorts of goodies, most of which I filched from various campers. Anyway, all of that is a long story.

The point is, those people found me camping at Blackwood Lake a few days ago. One of them claimed to be an artist. He said he wanted to paint a portrait of me. That's how it started. I'm not about to write what they ended up doing to me, though. I guess we're different in that way, at least. You seem to enjoy writing about horrible things, whereas I would rather push such matters far away from me, ignore and forget them.

Here's the thing, though. I'm still banged up and sore from what they did to me. They were a gang of sick, vicious perverts. I was on my way back to their camp (after recovering for a couple of days) to wipe them out (or die trying) when you ran into me and damn near cracked my head open.

You sure did slaughter those people.

So you have my gratitude on a lot of scores.

Also, I think you're cute.

Even if I don't "win any prizes," I know you're very strongly attracted to me. I've read your diary, right? Oh, excuse me, your journal.

I know everything!

So. Suppose we get together, you and me, and roam the wilds together?

If you think that's a good idea, put down the notebook right about now, get to your feet and yell "Come 'n get it!"

I'm watching.

I'll come 'n get it.

You won't be sorry.

RICHARD LAYMON

The Beast House has become a museum of the most macabre kind. On display inside are wax figures of its victims, their bod-ies mangled and chewed, mutilated beyond recognition. The tourists who come to Beast House can only wonder what sort of terrifying creature could be responsible for such atrocities.

But some people are convinced Beast House is a hoax. Nora and her friends are determined to learn the truth for themselves. They will dare to enter the house at night. When the tourists have gone. When the beast is rumored to come out. They will learn, all right.

THE BEAST HOUSE

ISBN 13: 978-0-8439-5749-5

Master of terror

RICHARD LAYMON

has one word of advice for you:

BEWARE

Elsie knew something weird was happening in her small supermarket when she saw the meat cleaver fly through the air all by itself. Everyone else realized it when they found Elsie on the butcher's slab the next morning—neatly jointed and wrapped. An unseen horror has come to town, and its victims are about to learn a terrifying lesson: what you can't see can very definitely hurt you.

ISBN 13: 978-0-8439-6137-9

RICHARD LAYMON

They call it Beast House. Tourists flock to see it, lured by its history of butchery and sadistic sexual enslavement. They enter, armed with cameras and camcorders, but many never return. The men are slaughtered quickly. The women have a far worse fate in store. But the worst part of the house is what lies beneath it. Behind the cellar door, down the creaky steps, waits a creature of pure evil. At night, when the house is dark and all is quiet…the beast comes out.

THE

CELLAR

ISBN 13: 978-0-8439-5748-8

"If you've missed Laymon, you've missed a treat!"
—Stephen King

RICHARD LAYMON

Many people have a hobby that verges on obsession. Albert Prince's obsession happens to be cutting people, especially pretty girls. There's nothing he loves more than breaking into a stranger's house and letting his imagination—and his knife—run wild. Albert's on the run now, heading cross-country, but he's not about to stop having fun....

A pregnant young woman, a teacher, a librarian, an aging Southern belle, a famous writer and a budding actress. All of them have troubles and all of them are looking for something in their lives. Unfortunately, what they'll find isn't necessarily what they wanted. What many of them will find instead is Albert and his very sharp knives.

ISBN 13: 978-0-8439-5752-5

To order a book or to request a catalog call:
1-800-481-9191

This book is also available at your local bookstore, or you can check out our Web site **www.dorchesterpub.com** where you can look up your favorite authors, read excerpts, or glance at our discussion forum to see what people have to say about your favorite books.

RICHARD LAYMON

For two families, it was supposed to be a relaxing camping trip in the California mountains. They thought it would be fun to get away from everything for a while. But they're not alone. The woods are also home to two terrifying residents who don't take kindly to strangers—an old hag with unholy powers, and her hulking son, a half-wild brute with uncontrollable, violent urges. The campers still need to get away—but now their lives depend on it!

DARK MOUNTAIN

ISBN 13: 978-0-8439-6138-6

"If you've missed Laymon, you've missed a treat!"
—STEPHEN KING

RICHARD LAYMON

Something deadly has come to town—a slimy, slithering . . . *thing* like nothing anyone has seen before. With its dull eyes and its hideous mouth, it's always hunting for a new host to burrow into, and humans are the perfect prey. But the truly shocking part is not what it does to you when it invades your body— it's what it makes you do to others.

FLESH

"One of horror's rarest talents."
—*Publishers Weekly* (Starred Review)

ISBN 13: 978-0-8439-6139-3

☐ **YES!**

Sign me up for the Leisure Horror Book Club and send my FREE BOOKS! If I choose to stay in the club, I will pay only $8.50* each month, a savings of $7.48!

NAME: _____

ADDRESS: _____

TELEPHONE: _____

EMAIL: _____

☐ I want to pay by credit card.

☐ **VISA**   ☐ **MasterCard**   ☐ **DISCOVER**

ACCOUNT #: _____

EXPIRATION DATE: _____

SIGNATURE: _____

Mail this page along with $2.00 shipping and handling to:
Leisure Horror Book Club
PO Box 6640
Wayne, PA 19087
Or fax (must include credit card information) to:
610-995-9274
You can also sign up online at **www.dorchesterpub.com**.
*Plus $2.00 for shipping. Offer open to residents of the U.S. and Canada only. Canadian residents please call 1-800-481-9191 for pricing information.
If under 18, a parent or guardian must sign. Terms, prices and conditions subject to change. Subscription subject to acceptance. Dorchester Publishing reserves the right to reject any order or cancel any subscription.